MARSHALL CAVENDISH CLASSICS

SAVING THE RAINFOREST
AND OTHER STORIES

Saving the Rainforest and Other Stories

CLAIRE THAM

Marshall Cavendish
Editions

First published in 1993 by Times Editions

This edition published in 2021 by Marshall Cavendish Editions
An imprint of Marshall Cavendish International

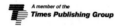

Other Marshall Cavendish Offices:
Marshall Cavendish Corporation, 800 Westchester Ave, Suite N-641, Rye Brook, NY 10573, USA • Marshall Cavendish International (Thailand) Co Ltd, 253 Asoke, 16th Floor, Sukhumvit 21 Road, Klongtoey Nua, Wattana, Bangkok 10110, Thailand • Marshall Cavendish (Malaysia) Sdn Bhd, Times Subang, Lot 46, Subang Hi-Tech Industrial Park, Batu Tiga, 40000 Shah Alam, Selangor Darul Ehsan, Malaysia

Marshall Cavendish is a registered trademark of Times Publishing Limited

National Library Board, Singapore Cataloguing in Publication Data

Name(s): Tham, Claire, 1967-.
Title: Saving the rainforest and other stories / Claire Tham.
Other title(s): Marshall Cavendish classics.
Description: Singapore : Marshall Cavendish Editions, 2021. | First published in 1993 by Times Editions.
Identifier(s): OCN 1253351028 | ISBN 978-981-4974-48-6 (paperback)
Subject(s): Rain forests fiction. | Self-realization--Fiction.
Classification: DDC S823--dc23

Printed in Singapore

Contents

Saving the Rainforest

I have known Ethel Png for twenty-five years now, ever since, at the age of fourteen, we were caned for wearing pink socks to school. It was 1966, the Western world was in turmoil, the Beatles were in the ascendant, and we were still in an environment where wearing pink socks was a major transgression. "I'm *dying* here," Ethel wailed to me more than once.

Not long after, her family, then one of the richest in Singapore, sent her to the United States to study. It was never clear *what* exactly she was studying, but she wound up in California, in the company of millions of assorted freaks, and began to "go wild," as her distraught mother put it to my mother. Ethel showed me photographs of herself back then, a small, even tiny figure, buried under an avalanche of hair that stopped somewhere around her kneecaps, and clad in exaggerated bell-bottoms a mile wide. She looked like Yoko Ono on a very bad day. Other photographs showed her sitting in a ring of similarly garbed people, all smoking joints. You could tell they were joints, because everybody had this fogged-out, loopy and yet perfectly ecstatic look on their faces. These pictures, which she stupidly sent back, threw her family into a tailspin and, in a fit of moralistic frenzy, they cut off her funds in an attempt to make her return. Instead, she started cultivating marijuana in her back yard in order to make a living, got busted, and languished in custody for a month, until her arresting officer, who was smitten with her, posted bail, after which they took off to Woodstock for the festival, of which she didn't remember a single thing. She did Woodstock, she did the lot: pot, junk, LSD, transcendental meditation, yoga, Zen, yoghurt, etc...

In 1972 her father was declared a bankrupt, the family money petered out, and Ethel was back in Singapore with a Eurasian baby christened Rainforest Peace Png, whom she called Rain. She said the father (her arresting officer) was a louse and a fascist who supported Nixon and she never wanted to see him again. Ethel's mother took one look at Rain, checked for signs of a wedding ring on her daughter's finger, found none, and promptly had hysterics. Ethel's father committed suicide, consumed with shame at the collapse of his business. Her mother eventually retired to a small house in Katong with the faithful family retainer, leaving Ethel with a mountain of debts and relatives who treated her like a pariah.

Meanwhile, my life continued its slow and enervating course. I read law at the local university, I had one or two boyfriends, nothing serious—earnest, steady boys who wore glasses. My parents went on being respectable, refusing to go mad or spectacularly bankrupt. Even though Ethel's life was clearly a mess, I could never see her without feeling a pang of envy: how could one person monopolise all the excitement rationed out on this island?

Ethel took a look at her situation and decided it was serious: she had an illegitimate son and no money. So she decided to put her Californian experience to some use: she started a health food shop. At that time, everybody thought she was making a mistake. They told her meat-guzzling, oil-slurping Singaporeans would stay away in droves, and they did, at first, but Ethel refused to admit defeat. A committed vegetarian herself, she wrote articles, pamphlets, appeared on TV, gave talks; at one time, it was impossible to avoid Ethel's face or voice, expounding on the benefits of lentils to the digestive system. Ethel's *Healthy Living* stopped being a mere curiosity shop as she began to see some return on her investment.

The only problem was that for years she never abandoned her uncompromising hippie lifestyle: she never stopped smoking pot, for example, which, in the anti-drugs hysteria then prevailing, led to her arrest (again), but the charges were dropped for lack of evidence. Magnanimously, she invited the investigating officers around for a vegetarian cook-out at her place; several of them, seduced by the great chilli stringbean recipe, no doubt, later became her lovers.

I thought she was completely mad and told her so.

"Darling, I've given up worrying what people think of me," she said. "You should try it—it gives you a marvellous sense of release."

But I knew I never would.

• • •

9

Rain was a large, solemn baby who never cried. He grew into a plump, stolid child with the unnerving habit of standing silently by your elbow while you talked on, unaware of his presence. He was watchful, unchildlike. Eurasian children are often said to be gorgeous, but there were no traces of it in Rain, who was ordinary, even homely. As far as I knew, he never asked after his father. When I asked him why, much later, he said, in a matter-of-fact way, "Because I thought Ethel *was* my father *and* mother." (He called her Ethel.)

Ethel and I kept in touch regularly, though by the time we hit our thirties we had become totally different people. At university, I had had visions of myself being gloriously martyred at the stake of legal aid, dispensing good in my best lady-of-the-manor fashion. After six years of unremitting drudgery, however, I had switched to corporate law, turning my back forever on the Causes, and was ready to do battle with anybody (but especially Ethel) on the question of selling out and joining the rat race. I worked long hours in the office and then worked out furiously in the gym, I kept my figure, and I shed the gawkiness that had so painfully accompanied me through my late teens and early twenties. After an early bad incident, when I had burst into tears before a senior partner after he had ticked me off, I made a vow never to parade my feelings before the world again. I put effort into mastering a cool, detached exterior; I learned that to say little except that which was pertinent could be an intimidating weapon. Behind my back, I knew, I was described as cold;

I counted it a victory. It had taken me years to reach this outwardly calm, emotionless pinnacle; I had no intention of ever climbing down again.

Ethel, true to her philosophy of doing precisely what she wanted and cocking a snook at the world's opinion, decided at age thirty-five she was going to let it *all hang out*, "including wrinkles and saddlebags on the thighs," she added cheerfully. She stopped wearing make-up and worrying about her weight, and she chopped off her tresses. Overnight she evolved from a flamboyantly dressy woman battling futilely with her figure to a crop-haired, kindly, chunky, mid-life person ("There is no such thing as middle age," said Ethel. "Middle age is a state of mind.") whose main concerns were saving the environment and her son, who was running around with a manic skateboarding crowd. Yet she was as attractive to men as ever, though some unkind persons were heard to say it wasn't possible, given the way Ethel clumped around. "It's my devastating earth mother quality," she would say, rolling her eyes, "I'm a terrific cook, I never interrupt those tiresome monologues men are so keen on—what more could they want?" But she had momentary regrets; once, scrutinising me carefully, she sighed. "You know, I could pass for your mother," she said wistfully. But at some deeper level she was at peace with herself now; tolerance for the world and its foibles oozed from her, thick as honey, comforting, and soon she was kidding me about my hair: "If I hit it with a hammer, what do you bet the hammer will break?"

• • •

You know it's downhill all the way when the children of your friends start to marry and you're still single. You start to feel unaccountably old—an imaginary pain starts up in your knee, you take out Procol Harum, *A Lighter Shade of Pale*, and play it to a nostalgic death on your turntable.

I was in no mood to go to the wedding of Lee Su Ting's daughter, the second in a month to which I had been invited. Su Ting's daughter Deanna (Deanna! for God's sake) at the ripe old age of twenty-two was walking down the aisle with the son of a timber merchant from Sarawak, and the ninny was delighted that she would be safely married before she was washed-up at twenty-three.

The wedding was being held in Deanna's grandfather's house, an old colonial bungalow set in, as the real estate brochures say, spacious grounds. I thought I would show myself, present the *ang-pow* and melt away before the service started; that way, I would avoid being inflicted with the unctuous "Till Death Do Us Part" rigmarole.

The young couple had been educated in England and had certain ideas as to how the whole thing should be conducted. They wanted to be married in the garden, under bowers and in the light of the setting sun, an idea which, in this climate sounded like sheer folly; luckily, it had rained in the afternoon and was considerably cooler. Deanna hugged me impulsively: "It's a shame, you're looking wonderful, when is your turn coming?" No less than four people asked me this question (her fiance, her parents, and her grandfather, whom I remembered from my youth as a keen lecher constantly inviting young girls into corners with him), at the end of which I was ready to stagger out and drown myself in the punch bowl.

I wandered off aimlessly into the garden. Someone waylaid me, wanting to know about a legal matter; I looked about desperately for an escape route, and it was then I saw a peculiar young man, hovering by the buffet table, eyes closed, lips moving silently. He was dressed entirely in black, black T-shirt, black jeans, black loafers. More than one person was looking at him in deep suspicion. He opened his eyes, saw me glancing at him, and came straight over, purposefully. "How are you?" he cried effusively, and bore me off on his arm.

"Wait," I said, struggling to free myself, "what are you doing?"

"Didn't you want to be rescued?"

"Yes, but I'm perfectly capable of doing it myself."

He released my arm. "OK," he said amiably. "You just looked terribly bored."

"Do you always rescue people who are bored?"

"Always," he said, gravely. "Life's too short to be bored. You should do something about it." Then he started to laugh, and couldn't stop. When he finally sobered down, he asked, politely, "So what do you do?"

"I'm a professional wedding gate-crasher." I amended this to, "Also a lawyer. And how old are you anyway?"

He looked at me as if I'd asked him something indecent. "Nineteen."

"For your information, I'm thirty-nine."

He shrugged. "So?"

"So I don't need someone who's practically a child rumbling in and oozing self-possession all over me."

He said nothing, except that his eyes narrowed and a rather tight look came over his face. I began to be sorry for what I'd said. "I didn't mean that exactly."

"Yes, you did," he said. "Why say things you don't mean?"

"Because a certain amount of hypocrisy is essential to a civilised life."

"Yeah?" he said, with a glint. "Well, screw civility."

I could have left, but some instinct of curiosity made me ask him what he had been doing by the table.

"That? Oh. Well ... praying for the souls of all the dead animals slaughtered for the occasion." He gave me a challenging stare.

"Oh, come on."

His eyes, a very light grey, bored into mine suddenly, illuminated by a stern joy. "That's just the lawyer in you speaking. Eternally sceptical. Only money, power, the things money can buy, are your verities, right? Hey, I'm not only a vegetarian—I've been one ever since I was born—but I know all of us living things are meshed together in this giant, interlocking organic whatchamacallit. You can't dislodge one piece without fucking the whole thing up. That's why I can't stand this century, man, it's a systematic attempt to de-harmonise the whole universe and deny the natural order of things..."

He went on in this vein for a full fifteen minutes, his eyes flashing, and his delicate, slender nose quivering, the whole complicated system of bones and muscles moving, shading fluidly in that narrow, angular face of his, his thin body held taut, whip-like, in his intensity. Periodically, he would flick the straggling, honey-coloured hair out of his eyes, then his hand would slide back into the back pocket of his jeans, his hands were always in those back pockets; even when he was standing still there was the indefinable hint of a light footed, cat-like wariness. He would never live from day to day, you could see that, he would always be hurling himself against some imaginary obstacle, carving his way furiously through the very air he breathed. He wound up with the air of having settled life, the universe and everything, with the arrogance of extreme youth, but he was smiling at his own seriousness, a lopsided smile stretching to his left ear.

"Your name's Rain, isn't it?" I said, when he'd finished.

"How did you know?"

"Oh, I know."

• • •

It was with some relief that I located Ethel in the sitting room, eating her way through a large slice of cake. "I've met your son."

"Oh, good," she said, vaguely.

"He's changed, hasn't he? I haven't seen him for years. He used to be such a fat child—"

"My genes," Ethel said, nodding.

"He's really rather—beautiful now."

Ethel gave me a sharp look. "Hmm." Meditatively, she crumbled her cake. "I don't know what to do."

"What about?"

"He's due to be called up for National Service soon. I'm not sure whether he should do it—you know he's still got American citizenship and he's got to make a choice soon between that and remaining here. It's not so much the dangers of army life I'm worried about. You know he's always been at one or other of the international schools here all along. I'm not saying it isn't my fault, but I just don't know how he's going to take to army discipline and all. You may have noticed he's rather strange."

Ethel, draped in a parti-coloured paisley smock and decked out in five-inch miniature Eiffel Towers for earrings, might have been described as being rather strange herself, but I forbore pointing this out.

The band in the garden struck up the wedding march. Ethel winced. "I suppose we should trot out for the nuptials. What a bore. Do you realise," she said thoughtfully, "I've never been married?"

"Neither have I."

"That makes two of us."

Ethel drifted out to the garden and I went to the back of the house to escape. But it was a large, rambling construction with odd corners and turnings, and I found myself instead in a long, high room, with a table piled high with wedding presents—or I suppose they were wedding

16

presents, since they were unwrapped. It looked as if some-one had raided the hardware and crockery departments of a store and dumped the contents, higgledy-piggledy; there was enough stuff there to equip five households at least and still have extra to spare. In spite of my determination to leave, I found myself drawn towards this unabashed display of materialism—not least because I had spotted a charming Royal Doulton figurine standing in the middle of the clutter.

I have a confession to make. I am an inveterate porce-lain collector. I am also mildly kleptomaniac. These two tendencies sometimes mesh, with unfortunate results (to the owners of the porcelain, that is), though I usually confine my thieving instincts to filching stationery from the office. I was single-handedly responsible for a memo circulated earlier this year, calling for frantic economies in office stationery. In case you think I'm being unduly facetious, I know I have a little—uh—problem, but I relish too much the irony of someone who's involved with the finer interpretations of the law being actively involved in transgressing it to give it up. I do it for the kicks, in other words.

It took barely half a second for the figurine to disap-pear into my bag. Turning to go, I saw Rain standing in the doorway, and froze. We were both extremely still for what seemed like a very long time; then he broke into a slow grin, and began to whistle. Slowly, I replaced the figurine and made my way past him, his black-clad body flattening itself against the door frame to let me through.

I felt, rather than saw, the amused, benevolent look on his face, the same irritating tolerance which Ethel brought to bear on the menagerie of freaks and downbeats she collected around her. I ran for the road.

As I was reversing my car, I glimpsed Rain, a tiny, black speck in the side mirror. Squinting, I could just make out that he was standing by an Alfa Romeo, eyes closed again, lips moving in benediction. What was he praying for now, salvation from the oil crisis, staving off global warming? That ludicrous, sanctimonious little brat. Then, as I watched, he picked the lock, jumped in and roared off with great verve, in a flurry of squealing brakes and screeching tyres. A thin echo of the Wedding March floated through the air.

• • •

Two days later Rain called me at the office to ask whether I would go with him to watch a Hungarian movie being screened by the Film Society. I said I never watched anything that had been mutilated by censorship, and, with this thoroughly pompous reply, hung up.

A few days after this, he woke me from my sleep at midnight to invite me to dinner with him. I said no. He said, why not? I lay awake for hours, staring into the dark.

I have one other vice. I watch movies alone. I need the luminous darkness of the auditorium, the plunge into another perfectly circumscribed universe.

As I recount all this, I'm aware I sound like a progressively dotty—what is it? Oh yes—*old maid*. Someone who spends time and effort cultivating her eccentricities like rare plants, rather than rearing a child. Ethel, for example, is fairly bizarre, a walker on the wild side, but because she's fathered—sorry, mothered—a son, she is somehow exonerated in the eyes of this society which sometimes sees women as nothing more than fertility symbols. Whenever I see one of those advertisements promoting happy graduate mothers and their babies, I feel so angry I have to restrain myself physically from smashing the television. To paraphrase the song, they're my genes and I'll squander them if I want to.

Anyway, I was talking about solitary moviegoing. In *The Moviegoer* by Walker Percy, the hero, who is searching for a meaning beyond his everyday existence, goes to movie after movie alone, a symptom of his disconnection from the modern world. It is a good book, but have you noticed it is always men who get to make these grand, angst-filled gestures? I don't pretend to be grasping after the meaning of life in a celluloid fantasy; I go alone because I'm old enough to enjoy my own company.

Sometimes I manage to stumble on an unexpectedly good movie as well. Or, in the case of *The Pope of Greenwich Village*, a good bad one, starring Mickey Rourke and Eric Roberts as a pair of Italian-Irish cousins who tangle with the mafia. Much of it was basically contrived, but I've always liked buddy-buddy themes, what with all that inarticulate emotion and sentimentality disguised as toughness. A kind of licensed homo-eroticism, if you know what I mean. Also, the cinema was almost completely empty, apart from someone snoring in the front row and a couple of people at the back—blissfully peaceful.

My only fear at these times is that I'll meet someone I know. It hasn't happened often but I hate finding myself in position where I have to explain why a thirty-nine-year-old woman is doing something as adolescent as sneaking into a cinema alone. Why don't I pair up with a VCR, if I can't find a man, I can feel them thinking—or perhaps it's just incipient paranoia on my part?

So you can imagine why my heart sank when I saw Rain outside. He *would* go alone, of course. He spotted me and came up, his eyes full of that lively, ironical curiosity I remembered so well from the day of the wedding. He suggested going for a drink and I found myself agreeing, guiltily caught in the second unsocial habit of my life. It struck me, not for the first time, that he was always catching me at a disadvantage—my God, it was enough to put anyone into a really foul humour.

Except that now his head had been shaved to an unbecoming stubble, and he was several shades darker, with a constellation of spots sprayed over his nose, taking a little of the bloom off that unnerving beauty of his. He was again all in black, a lupine, theatrical figure, and yet innocently natural within that theatricality. He touched each lamppost he passed—absent-mindedly or for luck? I asked him how he liked the army; he shrugged and said, "It's OK."

We went to a coffee-house, where I ordered an orange

juice and he ordered soup and salad. "You don't mind if I eat, do you? I'm starving."

"Salad's not going to fill you up, is it?"

Again that shrug. "It's the only vegetarian thing on the menu."

"Don't you want," I said, struck by an idea, "to pray for the souls of all the dead carcasses in the kitchen?"

"Not if you don't want me to."

"Are you always this intense?" I was baiting the kid, but I couldn't help it. "Do tell me what you want to be when you grow up—no, let me guess, a missionary, yes, that must be it, a visionary missionary, you have this desire to convert unbelievers—your only problem, as far as I can see, is finding a theology, unless Green politics fills the gap—"

"Hey," he said, breaking in, "I thought you liked me a *little*."

"What made you think that? You're Ethel's son, certainly, but I haven't seen you for ages. You were a very unfriendly child. Just as *intense*."

He wasn't listening. "It's this *age* thing, isn't it? It doesn't bother me, so why should it bother you? You know, this society, this world, just places too much goddamned emphasis on one's age. It's ridiculous. Age has nothing to do with it, unless you're a middle-aged guy, right, and you're sporting this little itsy-bitsy *doll* on your arm and everyone says, hey, you lucky dog, wish I could trade in *my* wife. (See, I've got impeccable feminist credentials— wow, three words with three syllables each at least.) You could be a hundred years old and I could be ten and I'd still like you. You're different."

"You know, you talk far too much, Rain. And you don't know what you're talking about. Believe me, I know, and I draw the line at younger men, especially very young men still living at home with their mothers."

"OK. I'm nineteen and you're thirty-something. So what? It's only a negligible difference."

"Only? Are you *completely naïve*? The gap is interstellar. *Intergalactic*. It's unhealthy. What you need is a cold shower. That will sober you up."

"Oh, come on," he said. "You talk about me as if I'm a sex-pervert-alcoholic-dope-fiend who's murdered his grandmother. I'm not. I'm a very nice guy. I love animals, I'm remarkably broad-minded for my age. I'm a bit pompous, but that can be cured." He grinned, taking the sting out of his words, and added, handsomely, "Besides, you're stunning to look at and everything. I bet lots of people must have told you that."

"No, actually they haven't."

"Besides, we were *born under the same star*."

"I *beg* your pardon."

He grabbed my hand suddenly. "Look, this is the lifeline ... it says you were born with a fatal weakness for expensive china and though you can afford to pay for it ten times over, it's more fun to relieve their owners of them ... anyway, they don't *care*, right...? And we could go to the movies together. We'll be together but we can pretend we went there alone."

I dragged my hand away. I was afraid of enjoying this too much and giving in to a crazy impulse to say yes. "No," I said. "Just eat up and let's go."

"OK," he said, throwing the napkin on the table. "Let's go." This little gesture relieved me a little; it gave me a concrete flaw to focus on.

He steamed to the cashier's. We paid our shares, and the cashier gave Rain a three-page receipt, each the size of his hand. Rain looked at the receipt and looked at the cashier. "What the *hell* is this? Why the *hell* is this place using three pieces of paper for one stupid receipt? Why *not*? I'll tell you why not. Because trees are a diminishing resource, that's why not. The rainforest is disappearing and no one gives a damn. We'll all go down in this sinking ship, gagged by waste-paper, smothered in dust."

His metaphors were becoming wildly mixed; I practically had to drag him out. "What is the *matter* with you?"

He sneaked a look at me, calm now. "I don't know. I'm a basket-case."

"Then get some help! Grow up!"

"I'm sorry," he said. "Really, I am."

I'm not sure why I didn't simply walk away from him then. Some nagging sense of responsibility, perhaps, or his gravely penitent air, which I didn't trust. "Come on, I'll give you a lift home."

He fell in step beside me. "Hey, I've thought of another argument."

"What?"

"In no time we'll all be dust and ashes."

"That's very comforting."

"Hurl yourself into the breach. No regrets."

We had reached my car by then. "I'll leave you here," he said. "I'm meeting some friends later."

"You didn't have to walk a geriatric to her car."

"I like walking geriatrics to their cars."

Oh, the corniness of it. Someone had catapulted me into a movie—that was it—a thrilling one, of mythic proportions, with my very own starring role, but which was rapidly hurtling towards a close; at any moment I expected the projector to shatter, the reel to fly out in whirling streamers. Experimentally, I placed my arms around him; it was like hugging a shadow, hard and yet somehow flickering and elusive. He tried to kiss me, but I wouldn't let him. Not yet, anyway. And yet I didn't push him away. I foresaw a lot of trouble. And ridicule. And an unpleasant, crepuscular old age as punishment. Why, oh why, can't we grow younger as we grow older? I felt something cold against his neck, a thin chain, with the words *Save the Rainforest* in silver filigree.

"What is this, your mantra?"

"Yeah," he said. "Rescue me." And he looked ecstatic.

• • •

What do you do in a relationship like that? A lot of the time was spent eating, or rather, watching him eat, as he was constantly hungry. Sometimes we went to the cinema but he was always so tired from training that sitting

24

down without the stimulus of food made him fall asleep instantly, head lolling against my shoulder. Once he dragged me into a bowling alley, a place I hadn't stepped into for years, where he practised obsessively until midnight, while a group of girls watched admiringly and I plotted his, and their, collective murders. But his curious mixture of sure-fire arrogance and infectious enthusiasm, so different from my own pallid teenage years, made me laugh, and I've never been able to resist anyone who made me laugh.

Some three weeks later came the telephone call I had been dreading; Ethel sounded cool and distant and aggrieved.

"I hear you've been going out with my son."

"Ethel. It was just for dinner."

"Really, I thought better of you."

"What has Rain been saying?"

"That he likes you."

"As a friend."

"Not *just* as a friend. In case you didn't know, he broke up with his girlfriend a month ago and he's rather restless and excitable."

"You talk about him as if he were a *puppy*. You know he's old enough to decide what he wants to do. Honestly, I thought you'd be wanting to protect *me*."

Long silence. "Ethel?"

"I'm too furious to speak to you now," she said coldly. "I called up hoping you'd deny everything, or that you'd act like a responsible adult. I'm going to make a tofu vegan meal—with lots of oyster sauce—and simmer down. Don't ask me for the recipe."

Now she was working me up as well. "Why this attack of conservatism all of a sudden? Gosh, when I think of all the times I could have told you you were making a fool of yourself ... I mean, you called him Rainforest, for goodness' sake! What kind of name is that?"

"That was then!" Ethel said. "This is now!" She hung up.

I was upset and the next time I saw Rain, I contrived to have a really big dust-up about Saving the Whale. I said it was all a load of virtuous hypocrisy on the part of the West while he turned white around the temples and I was thinking, why am I having this silly quarrel, I don't give a damn about whales, dead or alive.

"Ethel said she called you," he said at last. "That's what this fight is all about, isn't it?" (He and Ethel had one of those tiresome parent-child relationships where they thrashed everything out 'as adults', and in the weeks to come I began to feel I was going out with *both* of them, so indistinct did the line between Ethel/Rain and Rain/Ethel become. There's a lot to be said for the stiff upper lip, I feel.)

"All right." I said. "Partly. She's one of my best friends after all."

"Hey," he said, catching both my hands in his, "you don't think we're doing anything *wrong*, do you?"

Wrong? I had forgotten the meaning of the word. I continued to feel an intermittent guilt towards Ethel, but

I also had the curious sensation of stepping outside myself at times and watching this woman, whom I thought I knew so well, acting, behaving in a totally uncharacteristic fashion—but knowing that she was perfectly happy. Yes, glad, in spite of everything.

Occasionally, he was confined for the weekend, and then I became acutely conscious of the serried ranks of shaven-headed NS boys milling about Orchard Road, each, it seemed, with a very young girl clinging onto his arm; dear God, was I really degenerating to the level of those girls, waiting for a nineteen-year-old to be released by his sadistic commander or whoever it was? At moments the situation struck me as being so insane it was all I could do not to burst out laughing at the most inappropriate times, such as office meetings.

"I'm glad you see the ridiculousness of it," Ethel said, grimly, when I went to visit her at her shop; I hated the growing rift between us.

"Ethel, there's nothing going on."

"Then why are you wearing one of his shirts?" I looked down at myself. It *was* his shirt, a striped blue and white one: I liked its preppie, collegiate look. I had thrown it on without thinking, and I could think of nothing suitable to say now, though I was able to come up with a list of impressively innocent reasons later—by that time, of course, Ethel refused to listen.

"Excuse me," Ethel said frigidly. "I'm extremely busy." She was taking stock, and she moved efficiently, purposefully, down the shelves of muesli, cans of curried beans, raisin snacks, not the sort of thing I would ever want to eat, but I loved the genuine wooden decor of her shop, the folksy atmosphere, and the good, clean smell of wholemeal wholesomeness. Normally she would insist that we sit down and have some camomile tea and carrot cake, but today, I could see, was not going to be one of those days. Ethel wasn't the type to rant: her method was to practise a kind of biting reasonableness, with the intention of making you feel absolutely criminal. She almost succeeded, but not quite.

• • •

Surreptitiously, I devoured articles and books on my predicament. The gist of it, which I could see for myself, was that all the men my age were either married, gay, or, if single, appeared to have undergone a lobotomy. My only alternatives were widowers my father's age, younger men and *very* young men (a category growing every day), or a heroic celibacy—and I was prepared for neither the first nor the last. Yet I knew, rationally, that this thing with Rain was temporary; it was a fairy tale interlude, a glitch in reality—the end was already incipient in the beginning, and this, paradoxically, made me calmer, fatalistic, able to drift along without too much agonising self-examination. The people at the office remarked (maliciously?) that I was growing a softer look—at the same time as George Bush outlined his vision of a kinder, gentler nation, and the Cold War continued to thaw. Under Rain's influence, I threw out the cans of hair spray et al—full of CFCs, after all—though I kept the rows of night cream, body lotion, etc. on my dressing table, despite Rain's dogged eulogy of the Natural Woman. For a woman, nature has nothing comforting about it: it's a guerilla assault on her attempts to halt the onslaught of time. Besides, he was being disingenuous—I had no illusion that our attraction was anything other than largely physical, no matter how much he talked about a meeting of minds and idiosyncrasies; and physical attraction for a woman doesn't usually come cheap or unaided. Even feminists and environmentalists have their blind spots.

• • •

"How come you never married?"

"I don't know."

"Was it because of X?" X was the married man I'd had an affair with for eight years. I finally saw he would never leave his wife and that her tenacity was greater than mine.

"It's none of your business. Ethel had no right telling you."

"I'm sorry."

"Don't be. I'm glad to be out of it."

He played jazz saxophone sometimes in a band on Saturday nights. He said he had saved for years, helping Ethel in her shop, to be able to afford the saxophone—ever since he had been fixated, as a kid, by a picture in a book of a black jazzman, swathed in a zoot suit and wreathed in clouds of smoke. The picture had stuck in his mind, as a symbol of freedom and how-to-be-hip; even then he had, like his mother, an instinct for the iconoclastic and the offbeat. It was an odd ambition for a child to have, here, anyway, and indeed his whole life, apart from this shaky desire to play tenor saxophone and to save the world from eco-disaster, seemed to be ambitionless, shot through with a studied aimlessness that I didn't understand.

"What are you going to do after the army? Have you applied to go to university?"

"What is this, the Spanish Inquisition? You sound just like Ethel."

"You've got to decide what you want to do sooner or later."

He quoted the part in the Bible about the lilies of the field and how they toil not, neither do they spin etc., etc. I pointed out the flaw in his argument viz, that he was not a lily of the field.

"Power structures," he groaned. "That's all you're ever interested in, *power structures*."

"There's no scope for a Bohemian life here, in case you haven't noticed." He smiled, lazily.

So far I had avoided introducing him to any of my friends, and I had no inclination to meet any of his. "Are you ashamed of me?" he asked once, eyes glittering; of course I was. I also had the superstitious feeling, not easily explained, that if we met any third parties, the gossamer-thin basis of our relationship would simply disappear.

He kept asking me to watch him play, and it seemed

churlish to refuse continually. So I went down one Saturday night, unknown to him, about midnight; they were playing Thelonius Monk. It was one of those niche-in-the-wall haven concepts, where you practically sat with your knees jammed up against the back of the person in front and the cigarette smoke became a thick fog. The whole thing was so cool everybody onstage wore shades; I wondered how they saw enough to keep from tumbling off the minuscule podium. Rain recognised me, however, and raised his shades just the necessary fraction to give me a wide grin. He had a couple of solos, and got through them flawlessly; there were cheers and catcalls. Evidently, he had fans. Around one A.M. they bowed out, to lively applause, and a Filipino band took over. After some hesitation, I went round to the stage door.

The dressing room was so tiny I had the impression people were standing one on top of the other. There were about six of them, all much older than Rain, complaining about the horrible influence of jazz fusion on modern audiences: "Nobody wants to listen to the traditional stuff any more—" Rain rushed over and hugged me. "Hey, I'm so glad you *came*." He introduced me, not saying who I was. There was a chorus of hi's and they looked expectantly at Rain. He looked at me and for the first time since I'd known him, I noticed a glimmer of self-doubt.

"Uh, this is my aunt," he said, and ducked.

"You've got a really talented nephew here, Miss Whang. He's wasted in this place, wasted."

"Absolutely," I said.

• • •

Rain danced frenziedly around me, doing a distracting jitterbug as we walked along.

"I'll explain everything to the guys later. I'm going to kill myself."

"Forget it."

"I just sort of—blanked out."

"Rain, I would have done the same thing. I'm not angry."

"Well, I wish you would. Get angry. I hate this reasonableness—it's like my mother's moods, it means you're going to do something drastic later. *Please* get angry," he begged.

"I can't get angry to order." And then the hysterical laughter that I'd suppressed and that had been building up inside me for weeks suddenly bubbled to the surface. I laughed so hard I had to stop and catch my breath; the few people still about gave me anxious looks and crossed to the other side of the street. I laughed and laughed a lifetime's worth of frustrations. Rain gazed at me in astonishment, then concern, then, when I didn't stop, he walked further down and leaned against a pavement railing, arms crossed, not looking at me.

"I'm not laughing at you," I said, explanatorily, when I could speak again.

"Oh yeah?" he said, frowning.

Finally, when we had both calmed down, we went back to my place and made love. He said he loved me.

"I'm very fond of you, Rain," I said, truthfully.

"What do you mean, *fond*? You can be fond of a dog— or a stuffed toy. Come on."

But he was too tired to argue. I watched him fall asleep; I felt maternal, paternal, avuncular, the adult in charge of the situation once again. Then I got up noiselessly from the bed, so as not to disturb him, and padded to the kitchen, where I ate all the ice cream in the refrigerator.

• • •

Ethel called me again a month later.

"Hi," she said.

"Hello," I said, cautiously, formally.

She heaved an enormous sigh down the telephone. "I can't stay furious at you any longer," she announced dramatically.

"Really?"

"Yes, I don't have so many friends that I can afford to dispose of them like banana peel. Incidentally, did you know banana peel's wholly edible? I've got a marvellous recipe for it. Remind me to give it to you."

"I have to consider my options."

"Will you relax?"

I did, I was so glad to hear from her. "I was going to call you myself."

"Well, talk about telepathy."

"Ethel," I said, "I'm sorry."

"Hmm," she said. Pause. Rain hovered in the air between us, a phantasm. "You know he's talking about

33

going to California after the army, to look up his father, he says, heaven help him. The man probably supports Pinochet now. It'll give him a chance to decide whether he wants to stay on."

"Yes, I know. He says he'll probably enrol at a university there to do film studies and practise the saxophone."

"That layabout. Thank goodness the American government has to foot most of the bill." A little tartly, "And what will *you* be doing?" "Surviving, mostly," I said.

Sundrift

So many people had no idea how to dance, just stood around on the dance floor jerking inanely and self-consciously along to the rhythm. Clumping. Leena had no patience with them. Dance was a ritual, a ceremony; you had to learn the steps, patiently, or it was no good. With a tingle of malicious pleasure, she would fling herself into some complicated routine, knifing her small slender body through the throng; she loved it when a Latin-inflected song came on and the crowd thinned out, groaning, because the steps were too difficult, and she twirled into a flying patchwork of calypso, rumba, mambo, lambada—names that were wonderfully evocative and faintly absurd, while people would stop dancing to watch her, even to clap, and at the end of it she would give a deep, ironic curtsey.

• • •

She had noticed Steve the first night, leaning over the railing that separated the bar from the dance floor. She didn't think he was a guest at the hotel, of which the disco formed a part, or she would have noticed him sooner: she was the front desk receptionist. She knew he was watching her, and she liked the way he looked: tall, tennis-player lean and blonde, his hair just a tad too long and grazing the collar of his T-shirt.

She went dancing three nights in a row, and each time he was there, watching her. He knew she knew. She concentrated on him now, Salome-fashion, when she danced.

On the third night he moved towards her casually and asked if he might buy her a drink. She flicked her tangled hair out of her eyes.

"Why not," she said.

• • •

Of course, he had to be from California. Where else? California by way of Germany, where his parents were born.

"My parents were born in India," she said. "Kerala," she added, for his benefit, and of course it turned out that he had spent time in an ashram in India in the 1970s. It was too much. He reminded her of those assembly line actors in the American television series of her childhood: lanky in jeans, driving round in open-topped cars, vaulting fences, spouting cliches. Except that Steve never said much, letting her spin, like a whirlwind, from one topic to another. He was not as young as he'd first appeared to be; nearer forty than thirty, there were slight lines around his eyes and streaks of grey amidst the blonde. When he moved, his movements were like a cat's, slow and lithe and deliberate and sinewy. His low drawl was casual to the point of impenetrable.

He seemed to Leena inscrutable.

"Honey, I'm just an Oriental cowboy." She hit him, hard; she detected a lurking sardonicism.

• • •

"What are you doing out here?" She meant in Singapore.

"Business. Things."

He lived in an expensive condominium apartment and drove an expensive car. The apartment was in his name, starkly white and sparsely furnished, the austerity relieved by two gigantic abstract canvases in the sitting-room—curiously impersonal, and yet, curiously Steve. A Siamese cat called, improbably, Bhumipol, padded its way warily from one room to another, occasionally springing onto Steve's shoulder and nuzzling his ear, but leaping away with a diabolical yowl if Leena tried to approach it. She fully reciprocated its loathing.

"Such as?"

"Commodities. Raw materials. Import, export. I buy and sell stuff, set up deals, that sort of thing."

"Wheeling and dealing?"

"You could call it that."

"Ethical?" Leena said. "Or not?"

He grinned.

He had an office in one of the shopping centres to which he went at ten in the mornings and came back around three. Visiting the office once, she found it as spare as the apartment, with a single bored receptionist buffing her nails. She did not inquire further. In that respect, she feared, she had been culpable.

• • •

"Why is everything in your apartment white?"

"I'm a colourless person."

"White is a colour."

"No, it's not," he said. "It's an agglomeration of all colours. It's the negation of colour."

"Black is the negation of colour."

"Black is a kind of white and vice versa."

He was being deliberately wilful. She gave up.

• • •

Steve's friends were a wilder, ever changing crowd of expatriates, more rowdy and hard-drinking: oilriggers, seamen, jewellery dealers embroiled in litigation, various other people with ill-defined and probably dubious jobs. Leena suspected that one or two of them belonged in jail: the more charming they were, the more their criminality shone through, like a rash. They turned up on Saturday nights, uninvited, with crates of beer and stacks of country music records, great wholesome chunks of sentimentality to which they cried and stomped their feet along.

Like many expatriates Leena had met, they seemed oblivious to their actual surroundings, living, in their case, in a permanent mental American heartland frozen circa 1975. Vietnam was still an incendiary topic and opinions were evenly divided. One night, two men started a fight over the War, right in the middle of a Grateful Dead song; someone screamed, and Steve heaved a bucket of ice water all over the pugilists, who demanded, aggrieved, Wassa matter, man? And Steve said, Nobody interrupts the Grateful Dead. They claimed, all, to be flag-loving Americans "through and through," although none of them seemed particularly to want to go back: they were in hiding from ex-wives demanding arrears of alimony, governments demanding arrears of taxes; they were in the East because it was cheap and to "get their heads together." They talked, desultorily, about fleeing to Bali for good, they were caught up in the stream of their slow, rootless, restless drift around the world, a peregrination to nowhere. They believed, superstitiously and silently, that each new destination was another bead on a charmed necklace, the purpose of which, ultimately, was to stave off death: they were all, in the end, refugees.

Amidst all this unfocusedness, Steve moved through with the sharp, defined edges of a diamond; he was not in the drift, or so she thought.

• • •

They were married three months later.

• • •

Her parents were quietly horrified. Who was Steve? What was his history? What did he do? And where had she met him? Stiff with grief, as if someone had died.

They had never understood where her hoary streak of rebellion came from, her need to kick, mercilessly, at every perceived restraint. Changeling. Viper in the bosom. A tiny wisp of a girl in an otherwise ample family: any one of her brothers could have picked her up bodily with one hand. A mouth as wide and full-lipped as a jazz singer's, a pert, swinging walk seen at its best in short, flared skirts, a direct, challenging stare.

Her parents, nonplussed by all this sensuality, did their best to stamp it out. Leena was expected to be both a scholar and a traditional Indian woman, helping her mother with the chores while her brothers gambolled off. Chafing, Leena alternated between docility and outbreaks where she disappeared from home for days at a time. At eighteen, her truculent announcement that she was not going to university unleashed storms, her father (who ran his own law firm and believed firmly that life other than as a professional was not worth living) warning darkly that she was condemning herself to "a slide down the social ladder." Leena, unmoved, moved out: being the black sheep of the family was a draining activity.

But this was the decisive break—Leena and her parents both knew it. Leena had deprived her mother of the pleasures of matchmaking, of the noisy, triumphal excesses of a wedding; she had married a man who, in the orotund words of her father, had "the odour of too many scams about him." Again and again, her mother demanded to know: *why* this hole and corner business of popping into the Registry of Marriages one afternoon without informing anyone? Was she, heaven forbid, pregnant? Leena tried to explain: it seemed like a crazy, wonderful, impulsive thing to do! Her father said, swelling: crazy—wonderful—impulsive—we are not characters from a Victorian novel or a Hollywood romance!

Leena sat in the sitting-room of her parents' home, watching the clock on the wall. Two hours of heated discussion: nothing achieved, except mutual feelings of irritation and ill-will.

"Wouldn't you like to *see* Steve at least?"

"We never want to see that man."

A shade of doubt crossed her father's face at these words: even he seemed to think they sounded faintly ridiculous. But it was too late to recall them, they had been spoken. Leena said, "I'm sorry," and flew out of the driveway to where Steve stood, waiting, leaning against his car parked in the shade of a roadside tree.

• • •

The women of her family were fertile, if nothing else. Leena quickly found herself pregnant, and embarked on a voyage of unrelenting nausea, rollicking waves of it that made her feel as if she were at sea. She had to give up her job. Marooned in the apartment during the day, she was bombarded with calls from her family, entreating her to come home. But I want to be with him, she said, an unanswerable retort. She got the number of the apartment changed, twice, knowing that her family would be too proud to visit.

"There's no need to be so ruthless," Steve said.

"You don't understand," she said. Incapable of divided loyalties, she only understood partisanship.

Alone, she brooded, fitfully, on Steve. "I'm not an autobiographical kind of guy," he said once; at the time, she thought it a quaint phrase. She found that trying to glean information about his past life was somewhat like extracting teeth, a laborious, unyielding process. If she went too far, she could feel him recoiling, warily, and if they were in bed he would roll away from her and walk out to the balcony. There was always a final, inviolable territory to which he retreated and which no one could enter; she felt like an intruder for trying, even though she knew her questions were perfectly reasonable.

"Aren't they?" she said to Bhumipol the cat. "Isn't it reasonable to want to know a little?"

Strange thoughts occurred to her: perhaps Steve will be reincarnated as a green-eyed cat? And, I feel like a gangster's moll. Living in a zone of careful, studied ignorance.

She looked through his personal correspondence and his accounts when he was not there, but they were as unrevealing as Steve. When they kissed, it was as if they were sealing a pact of complicity—complicity in what, though, she couldn't say. And his unspoken resistance was wearing her down too; day by day she found it less and less unpalatable to accept him for what he was obviously determined to be, a fully sprung enigma.

• • •

She read in the paper one day that an American Vietnam War veteran, who had married a local Malay girl, had gone over the edge, kidnapping the children from his estranged wife and blowing his brains out in a messy suicide.

That night, troubled by a certain train of associations, she asked Steve whether he had ever been in the Vietnam War.

He laughed. Wouldn't stop laughing.

She grew annoyed. "Were you?" she persisted.

"Are you kidding? Come here." She settled, heavily, on the sofa beside him. Pregnant, she felt as large as an aeroplane hangar, ankles swollen and elephantine. "I feel ugly," she said disconsolately.

"Never," Steve said, his face buried in her tangled hair: barbed wire, she called it—she hated her hair. Taking hold of his wrist, she ran her fingers over the intricate bones, testing each knob; the pulse in his wrist throbbed, steadily, under the pressure of her thumb.

• • •

When the baby was born, they called him Ranjit. He was a tranquil baby who seldom cried, and seemed contained and self-sufficient in his cot, gurgling at invisible, friendly presences.

Leena cut off her hair and wore it close-cropped, penitential: she felt in need of a change after Ranjit's arrival. Depressed, intermittently tearful, she sat for hours beside the baby's cot, regarding him with the fascination she would have brought to the arrival of an extra-terrestrial: he looked like a cat, she thought, a large, unblinking,

43

hairless, skinned cat. (When she told Steve this, he said, worriedly, "Shall I call your mother?" And she snapped, "No!") She would start sewing clothes for the baby and, just as abruptly, would tear them up again. She remembered the French boyfriend, acquired at the age of eighteen, and how he had seemed to her so incomparably cultivated, until she had discovered he was seeing another girl. Then she had taken a pair of scissors to all his clothes. In moments of reverie, she could still hear the snip of metal tearing rents in cloth: a sweet, vindictive sound.

Steve said to her, "Are you going to be all right?"

She said, "Yes."

She wondered what she had got herself into.

• • •

In the beginning, she had liked the idea of it. Steve said he had business to do in various parts of Malaysia, that it involved a lot of travel over the next few months, and why didn't she come along? Leena was enthusiastic: she wanted, badly, to get away.

So they swathed the furniture in heavy covers, left Bhumipol with a friend, and piled, baby and all, into Steve's car one morning while the dew was still fresh on the grass. Wearing a red halter top and sun-glasses perched on top of her head, she looked so good that Steve insisted on taking a picture of her, which he did, and he stuck the Polaroid on the dashboard, for luck, he said; and when Steve rolled the top of the car down and the wind pinioned her to the seat and she could see the

44

Causeway approaching in the distance like a flat, grey snake swimming across the surface of the water to connect the two land masses, she was glad, glad, glad. She slipped her hand round Steve's neck as they sped on, and though he smiled, he continued to look straight ahead and not at her.

• • •

So began that somnambulistic trip.

Her memories of it were disjointed, like a film made with a jerky, hand-held camera: images skittered on and off, isolated names resonated.

Everywhere women in the Islamic headdress and men staring at her and Steve; she imagined silent strictures where there were none, then she grew indifferent. Everywhere the same small, dusty towns where the new and the decrepit stood side by side and the shops sold the chunky sweets which she remembered from her childhood in the same transparent plastic bottles on which the flies clustered thickly.

They stayed in the ubiquitous international chains in the larger cities, and in small family establishments of dubious cleanliness in the more rural places. Was it her imagination or was there a night when dozens of cockroaches crawled out from under their bed in the ramshackled Hotel Labuan and did a sort of jig in the middle of the floor, while she flew about, swatting them in her horror, while Steve said, drowsily, from the bed, that even cockroaches had the right to live?

And the time that the baby caught the flu, and it turned blue in the face from the fever and when they finally located the doctor, he pursed his lips and said they were mad to go tramping about the country with a new-born baby, didn't they know any better? And that was the only time she had seen Steve lose his temper, shoving the doctor up against the wall, unnecessary violence masking his—their—guilt, and they had had to leave town in a hurry, since the doctor was threatening a police report. The baby was fine in a few days, though.

Memory was a slippery, skidding thing.

• • •

Steve's 'business' consisted mainly of looking up various numbers in his diary and arranging appointments in every town. In the beginning, she accompanied him to these meetings. The acquaintance was invariably some Chinese man hoisting a handphone to his ear while his eyes raked Leena up and down curiously, and she glared back, defensively. In the larger towns, he wore a polo T-shirt and loafers and was called Johnson or Freddie; in the small towns he sloped into the restaurant (Steve's business was usually conducted over lunch) wearing slippers. They all seemed to know Steve from a previous incarnation: names of mutual friends, people she had never heard of, would be swapped with an artificial zest, the conversational equivalent of two boxers circling each other in the ring before a fight. Then they would suddenly descend to the nitty-gritty, talking in a cryptic code which Leena didn't understand and didn't bother to understand. (Her father had always deplored her lack of interest in money matters. Money, he liked to say, was the only vernacular in Singapore.) Calculators would be produced, and filofaxes, and impressively large numerals bandied about: sometimes the advantage would be with Steve, sometimes with the other man; it seemed to ebb and flow according to a barely understood law, indicated either by a discreet lift of the eyebrows or a crude banging on the table. All the while the Chinese man would urge Leena to eat, eat, a new mother needed sustenance, and if she said, no, she wasn't really hungry, he would look at her, frowning, and reply that he had ordered the best dishes in the restaurant. When she got bored, she would start reading, openly; finally, the Chinese man, unable to bear the provocation, would ask her what she was reading and she would show him the cover, with a creditable show of indifference. "No Harold Robbins, huh?" he'd crack, and she'd smile daggers at him and say, no, not today.

Steve said to her, "Do you have to be so childish?" She thought she might say to him, "Do you have to sup with the devil?" But she didn't.

So she took to walking around the streets with Ranjit propped in a sling across her shoulders, while Steve was out. People were friendly, Ranjit being a useful conversational tool, and they grew even friendlier when she practised her kindergarten Malay on them, making them laugh. Drifting from stall to stall, she would buy armfuls

47

of oranges, roasted corn on the cob, chestnuts, *kueh pinang*, and nibble her way through them with a furtive, guilty, sensuous pleasure. Coming back, Steve would find the hotel room strewn with half-empty bags and feign horror. He himself never seemed to eat, lived on a diet of salads, mineral water and bread, if that; he was getting ascetic in his old age, he said, only half-jokingly.

• • •

There was the time too that they woke up one morning to find a note slipped under their door saying, 'Get Out OR You'll Be Sorry', which she thought rather funny and clumsily melodramatic, but Steve had taken it seriously, going to the extent of questioning all the hotel staff about security: who was at the front desk the night before, didn't they see anyone coming in, what the hell, did they call this a hotel? By which time the staff were glowing with hostility and resentment, their faces closed in like so many fans snapped shut. And Leena standing in the background, pleading with him to drop it, it wasn't important, Steve, let's go. Seeing him as he must have appeared then: a crass, bullying American, a living justification for charges of neo-imperialism. Refusing to speak to him during the long ride to the next town, all four, dusty, bone-shaking hours of it, except to ask, Steve, do you have any enemies? And knowing then, knowing always, that he wasn't going to answer that.

It was best in the beach resorts, where she could lie on a towel on the sand all day, leaving the baby with the hotel baby-sitter, while Steve went off to town. Through half-closed lids she contemplated the shimmering bay, fringed by wooded hills, with a slight sense of misgiving that such unaccustomed physical beauty could exist, while all around her the mostly European guests baked themselves insensible, white maggot flesh metamorphosing into a blotchy lobster-red: her own skin ached for them in commiseration. When she could summon up the energy, she would take the launch out to go snorkelling (what a word, it sounded like a combination of snorting and snivelling). What did the fish see, she wondered, a gigantic behemoth with a face-mask goggling at them from the surface of the water? Letting her body go inert, limp, while they swarmed trustingly around her, and suddenly she would flail, faking a seizure, and watch them dart away in uncomprehending terror.

• • •

Once, he left at nine in the morning and failed to be back by four, as promised. She sat bolt upright in the hotel room, her eyes fastened with a painful concentration on the hands of the clock on the wall. She felt chained to it, every second ticking past a slow, corrosive drip on her patience; it snapped, finally, when Steve stepped into the room at midnight and she flung a book at his head and burst into wild sobbing. It took him a long while to calm her down, apologising all the while, rocking her back and forth, and gradually she stopped shaking and lay in his arms, docilely, while he stroked her hair, very gently, as though he were stroking some wounded animal. Later, she would think of that night as the night that he had unwittingly broken her in, like the horses he had broken in as a boy on his father's ranch; and she no longer remembered, not caring to remember, a life before Steve.

· · ·

In Penang, she befriended an elderly German couple, peeling valiantly in the sun. Childless themselves, they made an extravagant fuss over the baby, who had developed a predilection for rolling his tongue. "Gr-r-r," he would say, menacingly, tiny fists clenched, and they would look at him in unbounded admiration.

"And how long have you been travelling, my dear?" the German woman asked Leena over lunch.

"Four months."

"With a baby? Oh, that is too remarkable. And how do you manage?"

It hadn't occurred to Leena that there was anything to manage. "I like change," she assured the other woman.

"And how old are you, my dear?"

"Twenty-three."

"Yes," the German woman said, musingly, looking at her with what Leena surmised, with some resentment, to be a look of pity.

When she told Steve about this conversation, he grew annoyed and said they had to leave; he didn't like people interfering.

"She wasn't interfering. And I like it here." But Steve was already packing. She maintained an ominous silence. Passive resistance.

"You know,' she said, "I'm beginning to have my doubts about you."

"Only now?" Steve said, drily. He glanced across at her. "Honey, you're watching too many of those TV movies. I promise you I'm not a psychotic killer or a Bluebeard or a guy who secretly likes little boys, OK? This is just how I make a living."

"So what is your living?" She lay back on the bed. "You're always so *mysterious*. What am I supposed to think?"

"I'm a very ordinary guy," Steve said, ironically or not, she couldn't tell.

• • •

Clichés, she thought. Stars, hundreds of them spangled with a lush carelessness on a black canopy, hundreds of hackneyed phrases and trite sentiments slewed across the night sky; she had never realised there were so many before. It's the reflection of the city lights that obscures them and makes them invisible back home, Steve said, and she replied, sleepily, oh yeah? as she settled back on the cool, night sand. The tide was coming in in the dark, the water's edge marked by phosphorescent pinpricks of light, a wavy, luminescent hem. Wrapping her arms around Steve, she imagined she was embracing some long, hairy, unknown animal, a whippet, perhaps; the thought

51

amused her. A civet, Steve whispered in her ear. I've always wanted to be a civet.

• • •

Two weeks later, her nightmare began. Steve left for one of his interminable meetings and failed to return by nightfall. He had taken the car, or she would have driven out to look for him. She told herself not to panic: he would be back by midnight, like the last time, and she would kill him, then fling herself on him in exquisite relief. Sitting in the lobby in dark glasses, she ordered one daiquiri after another, losing all sense of time, until a waiter told her that the bar was closing. One A.M.

She went back to the room and lay down on the bed, fully dressed. Alcohol-numbed, she drifted off, dreaming fitfully of a splintering sun falling in a shower of ragged sparks to earth. A door banged in the corridor; asleep, she said aloud "Steve?" At dawn, dry-eyed, she watched the sky brighten, like a reddening weal, and made up her mind to go to the police.

The police failed to take her seriously at first. Yawned, unimpressed, in the middle of her recital. Called, impatiently, for coffee to erase the lingering traces of early morning inertia. Seemed to think that Steve, like many Caucasians in the town, had probably visited a local flesh-pot and overstayed a little. Murderously, in the tone of voice meant for an idiot-child, she said, "But I'm trying to tell you Steve isn't like that."

Desperate to shake their apathy, she drew out some

money from her purse and laid it on the table. Their faces rumpled with indignation. Was she trying to bribe them? She shrugged, and for a moment it looked as if this gaffe had thrown the fragile state of bilateral relations between their two countries into the breach, when one of the officers, relenting, wordlessly gave her a form to fill in.

It was a missing persons report. "Eyes," she read. "Hair." "Height." "Race." She checked it twice to make sure she had left nothing out, then settled down on the one hard bench in the station to wait. An officer suggested to her that she should wait at the hotel, but this elicited such a wild, swivelling glare that he retreated hastily.

• • •

Six hours later, they fished Steve's body out of the river. He had been stabbed cleanly—if cleanly was the word— through the heart. The wound was barely visible. It was clear that he had died before being heaved into the water. Attempts had been made to tidy up the body before she was asked to identify it at the mortuary, but a discoloured strand of seaweed was still strung, like an incongruous tribal decoration, around his neck.

• • •

"Suicide?" the police inspector hazarded, hopefully, pencil hovering above the stack of forms he had to fill in. Leena felt an impulse to scream, to smash something, rising up unbidden; only the thought that there was no one to hear her—no one who really mattered—constrained her.

She was telepathically aware of an unspoken, insidious, floating suggestion that Steve's death was more of an administrative nuisance to the police than anything else. If they could have closed the file on Steve Bauer, they would have done it with a smart click and an exhalation of relief.

"I want an autopsy," she insisted. "He was *murdered*. Do you hear me?"

Her vehemence was such that the inspector adroitly removed all sharp objects (mainly pencils) from her vicinity. Sighing paternally, he pointed out they had no leads. She had no idea what her husband did, whom he had gone to meet. His diary was missing. They would do their best, but really—he gave another shrug, wonderfully expressive of a resigned fatalism. "You should go home, Mrs Bauer."

Leena tried to call her mother in Singapore from the hotel, but no one was answering. Replacing the receiver, she was startled when the telephone burst into shrill, ringing life: it was the mortuary, wanting to know what her plans were.

"Plans?"

"For the disposition of the body."

"I'm sorry, I can't think right now," Leena said.

A pause. "Well, we *are* running out of space..."

She left the phone dangling, and, sweeping Ranjit up in her arms, fled to the beach. The afternoon sun had the intense white brilliance of a magnesium; she felt blinded, bludgeoned by the light. The fine powdery sand ran over her toes and burned the soles of her bare feet.

Fully-dressed, Ranjit asleep against her shoulder, she walked into the sea, kept walking, until the water covered her waist, and stood, irresolute, looking towards the horizon.

Deep Sea Sloth

Jek has just turned seventeen. He has shot up in the last few months: that sudden spurt of growth has fined out his frame and wrought a subtle transformation. I am aware that he simply does not look like other boys his age, though it would be impossible for me to pinpoint exactly this niggling difference. Feature for feature, he is ordinary, surely: clear, questioning eyes that reproach me for my cynicism, shaggy hair that flops into his eyes and over his collar, despite his mother's entreaties that he get a haircut, nose, ears, chin, like everybody else's. Yet, not quite like everybody else: I see heads turning to look at him when he walks down the street, girls' especially, but he seems oblivious to the attention, or at least I hope he is.

I believe in the sanctity of the ordinariness of every-day life: beyond its charmed boundaries lies confusion. Confusion, a sense of being under siege, are what I remember from that restaurant dinner when a man came up to our table and insisted on giving us his card. He said he was a professional photographer who was always looking for interesting faces. "Those cheekbones," he said, euphorically, "those planes, is 'sculpted' the word I'm looking for? It's perfect." We looked at him as if he were mad. Jek turned bright red, and my wife's hand closed, instinctively, over his. "He's only a child," I said in anger, rising. The man backed away, hands flung up defensively before his face: "Hey, no offence, man." The other diners were staring, cutlery poised in mid-air. Jek turned on me, outraged: "Dad, I can take care of myself!" "Ssh," my wife said. We finished our meal in silence.

• • •

When I was Jek's age, I was acne-ridden, bad at games, awkward around girls. It took me years as an adult to stop feeling self-conscious about myself, to stop feeling that my body had been foisted on me in an experiment gone awry. I watched Jek with a certain envy; I watched his skill at games, his uncomplicated ease, his facility with girls, and I waited for some cautionary lesson, some adolescent trial to surface, but it never did. Jek steamed on, unruffled, unvanquished.

Life was too easy for him, I thought: he needed privation, deprivation, a spell of living on bread crusts and water, some long hard grappling with the soul in the depths of night.

My wife ridicules my notions; in fact she gets livid whenever I air these views. My wife is a psychologist who believes in the untrammelled development of the individual (i.e. let the kid run wild).

"You don't know how hard life was for your mother and me," I tell him. "We came from large families; we never had anything new; we knew the value of hard work."

Jek rolls his eyes, says, "Yeah, yeah, yeah, yeah," acting hugely bored. His new word for me is *fustian*: "It's sort of Old English for square."

His latest girlfriend is called Siew Ping. Her waterfall hair screens half her face and has to be flicked back, constantly; on her first visit she told us she wanted to be a merchant banker because it was a growth area in financial services and would I, as someone working in a merchant bank, give her a few useful tips? She seemed at least a decade older than Jek.

Jek admits he isn't too enamoured of Siew Ping himself; she is too energetic and ambitious for him. Lately, he has been overcome by bouts of inertia and has taken to lying on his bed, refusing to get up for dinner, refusing to take calls. "I'm having a withdrawal," he says, if we ask him what the matter is; and if we ask, withdrawal from what, he says, dreamily, "Life." (His real withdrawal is from his mother and me; he has become—not secretive, but the days when he would burble on happily about his feelings—he was, if anything, a fledgling narcissist—are over.) This sort of behaviour drives me wild, and Jek knows it: he wants to see how far he can push me.

"You know what I want to be?" he says. "One of those deep sea creatures that never see the light and inch across the ocean floor. A sort of deep ocean sloth."

How can anyone fail to find him engaging? Nobody understands what I mean when I complain about his deliberate perversity, the delight he seems to take in thwarting me. By complaining, I appear like a mean-spirited curmudgeon. I love my son, but I feel we are engaged in an hourly, unspoken tussle that can only end in complete victory for one of us; compromise is out of the question; yet if I were asked what the nature of that tussle is, I would be unable to give shape or word to it.

His best subject is English. My greatest fear is that one of these days he will come and tell us that he wants to be a writer, and I will be obliged to be, as he says, *fustian*.

• • •

Frank Ying was the colleague I knew least of all, a quiet, rather moody man who smoked heavily and was always the first to arrive in the office and the last to leave. We knew he was married, but he seldom mentioned his family, and that set him a little apart, in an office where we bragged, unashamedly, about our families. He told me once, casually, that he had seriously contemplated joining a religious commune in India; when I asked why, he replied, flippantly, "Oh, celibacy." Despite his obvious competence, he had been passed over, repeatedly, for promotion; the consensus among top management was that he was too much of the analytical intellectual, lacking in a certain basic ruthlessness. Yet Frank stayed on, though we often wondered how he felt about being undervalued.

Not being close to him, I was surprised when he came over one day and suggested that we go for lunch. "Sure," I said; I guessed it was to vent his frustration over work and to ask me about his future in the bank; I have had several of these lunches before.

We went to a Japanese restaurant where I discovered that Frank, among other virtues, could speak Japanese. He said he had spent a year in Japan in his youth.

I said that, with his myriad interests, he was wasted in the bank.

Frank never misses a nuance; he smiled, wryly. "I like working in the bank, you know," he said. "I like the work. Advancement doesn't mean that much to me."

"Well, as long as you and your family are comfortable."

"What?—Oh, yes." He fell silent, again retreating into his taciturnity.

Then, unexpectedly, he asked me whether I had ever been to a certain nightspot notorious for being an expensive pick-up joint. I said, no, and ordered some sake. If this was going to be one of those conversations, I needed ballast.

He had gone there to pick up someone, anyone. He said this matter-of-factly (as if I were privy to this sort of reckless desperation): his marriage had been over for some time, his wife and son had gone back to her parents in Malaysia.

"I'm sorry," I said.

He brushed this aside; it wasn't what he wanted to talk about.

• • •

I don't (he said) go to these places as a rule. I don't like the searching scrutiny, the intensity of which can make the back of your neck shrivel: men scrutinising women, women scrutinising men, under cover of their bright, senseless, machine gun patter, patter which they have used all day in the office and find it hard to discard at night, patter which becomes frozen in predictable channels over long, cool drinks with silly names.

I don't remember what I was thinking that night, something about my family, nothing I could articulate: all I knew was that I had this black dog of depression clamped, remorselessly, on my shoulder. I get these attacks sometimes and there's a physical texture to them, something grey, viscous, damming up my lungs and vision. Do you know some psychologists think that depression can be a creative force, that it was probably one of the sources of Churchill's genius? I've never believed that to be true, except of inherently creative people. If you're like me, just some office worker who sits in a refrigerated little box from eight to eight every day, there is nothing fruitful about depression.

I started observing the crowd; I like observing people, it gives me the illusion I'm outside of myself for once, free of the burden of self-consciousness. There was a party of teenagers in a corner, which was unusual, because it's not really a gathering place for them, the prices are too steep. They were trying to order alcohol, even though it was clear they were all under the age limit; they thought it uproariously funny to make the waitress repeat, over and over, "We don't serve alcohol to minors." And they would hoot, "*Minors!*" and fall about, laughing. They were making too much noise, their crass, unbridled effervescence a direct affront to all the brittle cheer that the adults around them were faking. They were middle-class kids, you could see that, the bright, articulate, prematurely sophisticated, terribly immature type, the type that got to use their parents' credit cards and were allowed to drive the old man's car on weekday nights. A few of the girls sat on the boys' knees and there was a lot of playful cuddling and squealing—kind of touching, really, they were so young and unknowing, despite their assumed adultness.

There was one boy who sat facing me directly, his head slumped on the shoulder of the girl next to him, a little distant from the general boisterousness around him. He was a good-looking kid. It wasn't some vacuous perfection; he had an interesting face, some quality that made you pause and look again, something of the hooded austerity of a monk and the canny knowingness of a street hustler, something intense, ascetic, wary. Do I sound crazy? I can't describe it, him, very well. All I knew was that I wanted to take that face between my hands and kiss its forehead, its eyelids; I wanted to run my fingers over its contours, as I would a sculpture.

I see now you want to ask me about my marriage, the question hovering on your lips, is that why—? I can't answer that. Possibly. I don't know. I've never admitted it to myself and it's not something that would occur to my wife, whose innocence would be touching if it weren't so lethal.

To be honest with you, I'm not particularly interested in sex with either sex. My wife was the only person I slept with in the first thirty-five years of my life; there were two others, both women, both one-night-stands in Thailand before the happy advent of Aids. Not that I haven't wondered what it would be like with a man, except that I have no idea how to go about it, how I would recognise another man like me if I met him. That, and the fear of being identified with the ultra-feminine boys in school who had always repelled me with their graceful, swaying walk and talk of lipsticks and eyeshadow. Of course I realise there is an element of self-hatred in all of this: that if I am what I am (which I do not yet admit), then I am no better, or worse, than what those boys are. Yet we persist in drawing ridiculous distinctions in the face of logic or decency, in claiming a monopoly of virtue, masculinity. I am no better, or worse, than anybody else when it comes to blind self-righteousness.

But that night I thought I saw a glimmer. Not sex, not physicality, I simply wanted some connection with that strange boy. I wanted, very intensely, to know what he was like. What games did he play, what school did he go to, what did he want to do in life, which books did he read? My main emotions were curiosity, and, yes, a very distinct excitement. The sort of excitement you would feel if you had been searching for something all your life and it dropped into your hand, suddenly, with a reproachful clatter at your lack of faith.

I had no idea how to approach him, though, in the middle of that crowd, and I thought I would surely go mad unless I spoke to him; I had this palpable need to *see*, to *hear* him.

And then, incredibly, he looked at me, saw, I suppose, this incredible, despairing need, took pity on me; or perhaps he was curious too, just like I was—I sensed he was probably used to people staring at him, appropriating him, seeing him as a commodity to be savoured, tasted. What is it about beauty that puts it in the public domain, that makes you and me feel freely entitled to it? He said something to his friends, and, unbelievably, he was walking towards the bar, where I sat, he was taking a seat next to me, his eyes never leaving mine.

With that same incredible self-possession, he said, "You could buy me a drink." He spoke simply, even seriously. I think he was testing me, to see whether his instincts had been right.

I said, stupidly, that he was a minor. He said I could pay for it and he could drink it, and so I did; I don't remember what it was, but he gulped it down in one shot and gave me this brilliant, watchful smile.

"You're scared," he said.

"Yes," I said.

"You want to go to bed with me, don't you?"

My mind went blank; his nearness, his audacity, seemed to be muffling my thoughts.

"Yes, I think so, probably," I said, idiotically.

He said, simply, "Well, then, let's go."

And I followed him out of the door. I expected his friends to call out to him, but they didn't, although there was one girl who was watching us like a hawk, the girl whose shoulder he had been leaning against, a girl with long hair falling over half her face and which she clawed back, distractedly, from time to time. I felt her gaze at my back, even as the boy and I left, I felt it all the way to the car park, even as I was watching the boy stride ahead of me. She knew, I don't know how, but she knew, and she would have willingly killed me out of that age-old, maternal protective instinct for the young. (He had a funny, loping walk, a sort of quicksilver cat burglar prowl, leaning slightly forward on the balls of his feet.) And then, as we drove off, and the unfamiliar, miasmic quality of the enterprise overwhelmed me, I forgot the girl and her furious, unblinking gaze.

In the car, he sat low in the seat, long legs bunched up against the dashboard; he said nothing, looking straight ahead with that unsmiling concentration, as if he were tracking his own distant star. His silence unsettled me. I've never been able to bear another person's silence, though God knows I've been accused of the same unnerving trait myself, and I started talking to plug in the silence, before it suffocated me.

I told him about Clara. The usual, and not so usual, story. We married young, in a curious coming together of fatalism on my part and a desire to escape home on hers. Fatalism because I knew I had to get married, it was one of the things you had to do. I wanted to get it over with, all because I had to prove to myself that I could want a woman, live with a woman. We went into it with the ruthless practicality we would have brought to a business transaction, except that neither of us knew that this passionless beginning would erupt into a passion of tears and recriminations that was like being edged nearer the brink of death every day. Clara with her demands for attention, her wanting a part of me which wasn't there, which I couldn't give...

And I watched myself falling deeper into the morass with every despicable thing I said about Clara, and for what? To propitiate this boy who didn't seem to be listening, and if he were listening was probably doing so with a youthful, weary contempt, vowing to make me pay for inflicting this utter, utter banality on him.

In the end, I stopped talking altogether, and he said, "Nice car. How much did you pay for it?" and he ran his fingers, appreciatively, over the fittings.

He wasn't intending to be cruel; by the lights of his sheltered world, he was being polite by doing me the favour of asking me about my car.

I told him. I had the sensation I was having one of those fabled out-of-body experiences; I had become a speck on the ceiling of the car, watching my physical self go through these contortions, asking ridiculous questions: "Do your parents allow you to be out so late?"

"My parents?" he said, slowly, as if he had never heard of this concept before. "No, I guess not."

"Won't they be worried?"

"Hey, if you did everything they wanted you to do—"

"You'd be a better person."

He looked at me, frowning. "What do you do for a living?"

"I work in a bank."

"So does my father. He's senior vice-president."

"So you're a nice, well brought up, upper-middle-class child."

"Are you trying to make fun of me?"

"Heaven forbid."

"Do you mind not calling me a child? My father does that all the time and I can't stand it."

In the house, he wandered about, touching objects with a wondering curiosity, refusing my offers of food and drink; he seemed completely at ease, except for that flickering, watchful quality in his gaze, which came and went from time to time. Anybody watching us might have concluded that he was the host and I the interloper, a blundering moth that had strayed in from the dark. My home looked different to me, distended, askew; and I was cold, unaccountably cold, hands numb, feet numb, shivering slightly.

He paused, finally, before a photograph of my family on the side-table. "Is that your son?"

I said, yes.

"How old is he?"

"Eighteen."

For the first time that night, he looked at me as if I

had come alive, flickered into reality, for him.

"I'm seventeen," he said, fingers tracing, perhaps unconsciously, the face of my son in the photograph.

I wanted to die, I assure you, and yet I had never felt so keenly, glitteringly alive: every moment had a sharp, faceted, diamond clarity.

"I want you to understand—I don't normally do this sort of thing."

"Do what?" he said, very deliberately, wanting to pin me down, a wriggling insect, to watch me squirm. Then absolving me: "You don't have to explain anything to me."

He came and perched on the armrest of the sofa on which I was slumped; he was so near I could smell his young warmth, smell the freeze-dried, crackling, acrid smell of cigarette smoke in his clothes, his hair. I knew what he was thinking—you don't believe me? He was thinking that if he were to leave now, walk out of that door, I would be hugely relieved, would dismiss this whole episode as a reprehensible, but forgivable, lapse. And he was considering doing it, considering being kind; considering whether he had it in him to be kind, he was not an unkind person, no, it was just that it was still a novelty for him to discover that he could put people so completely in his thrall, hold them captive in the palm of his hand, just by their looking at him and wanting him, wanting him with a desperation that was alien and a little repellent and yet not unflattering to him—he was flexing, testing that power, in a pure spirit of experimentation. In ten years, five, he could be a monster of manipulation,

68

but that night there was still something artless about his attempts at learning how to walk.

He touched my shoulder, lightly; I flinched, went still. His hand crept up to my neck, began a gentle, caressing motion. I closed my eyes; a sort of lassitude had taken hold of me; suddenly, I wanted, very badly, to sleep, to fall asleep with him next to me; and then his hand was sliding into my shirt, and I felt his lips on my neck.

And then I was pleading with him to stop, which he did; and with an effort I removed his hand, kissed it, let it go.

"What's the matter?" he said. "Why are you crying? Didn't you like it?"

I answered his first two questions. "I'm drunk." The embarrassing tears were trickling, salty, into the corners of my mouth.

"No, you're not," he contradicted.

"No, I'm not."

I tried to light a cigarette, but my fingers were trembling too much. Wordlessly, the boy leaned over and did it for me. He lit one for himself too, watching me all the while with that unceasing wariness, leavened, now, with genuine curiosity.

After a while, he said, "You're ashamed, aren't you? Or you think you ought to be."

"Why are you doing this?"

He didn't answer. I asked him again.

"I'm bored," he said. "Bored with life, bored with family, bored with girls, bored with everything."

"Your life must be too easy."

"That's what my father says."

"Your father and I probably have a lot in common."

"Look," he said, "I have to go."

I grabbed his hand. "Why are you doing this?"

"Look, I have to get back."

"I'm talking to you."

"Kicks," the boy said. "Can I have my hand back?"

"Kicks? You're too intelligent."

"My father has my life mapped out for me," he said. "'A' levels, medical school in America, specialisation in some field, probably gynaecology, because that's where the money is. I dream sometimes that my father's holding me down by the throat while the waters close over my head."

"Very dramatic," I said. "Very banal. I don't believe a word of it."

He sighed. He looked faintly disappointed, sulky, as if the evening had elided into the farcical and he wanted to call a quick halt to the proceedings; the sulkiness brought back the hint of the self-absorbed child that he must have been not too long ago. I seemed to be seeing him for the first time, and what was he? A moderately attractive teenager, with a face I now recognised—brazen, yes, but not dangerous, not extraordinary, not incandescent. No. That heightened sense of madness which had flooded me when I saw him was draining, ebbing; I was tired.

"Look," he said, "I have to get back."

"What do you want to do instead?"

He hesitated. "I want to write."

At that point I began to laugh.

"You won't write about this, will you?"

"I probably will," he said, coolly.

"You know, you should be more careful."

He smiled then. "What, serial killers and stuff?"

"Among other things."

"I can take care of myself."

"You're very strange, you know that?"

"Speak for yourself," he said, equably.

"Come on," I said, "I'll send you home."

And he followed me, obediently, to the car. He was asleep by the time I backed the car out of the driveway, waking up only when I deposited him, yawning, at his front gate. He slept the sound, impregnable sleep of the exhausted and the just, curled up like a baby in his seat, and there was in his sleeping figure that same trusting, reckless abandon with which he had walked up to me and asked me whether I wanted to go to bed with him. I no longer wanted to touch him; he had become as remote and obscure as one of those surreally beautiful people on screen, whose existence you fail to believe in even when you see them, tenuously real, in the flesh.

He never asked me how I knew where he lived.

• • •

"It's strange, isn't it," said Frank, "that the same genes can produce such different results in different people. He does look like you, you know. Yet—not like you."

"I've always thought it was less trouble to be ordinary," I said. I seemed to have difficulty swallowing my food.

"What's his name?" Frank said.

I told him.

"Of course, you'll accept my resignation."

"Please," I said, "let's not be melodramatic. You just said you liked your work."

He said he wanted to take a year out to travel and to think. I told him, as I felt bound to do, that this would be suicidal behaviour, no organisation would re-employ a man in his middle forties who did something so impulsive; and yet recognising that perhaps this was something he should have done long ago, Frank was not a corporate man or a team-player or interested in getting up the learning curve or indeed in jargon of any sort, and never would be. We argued back and forth, skirting the real issue that lay just beyond the parameters of our conversation, until I was reluctantly prevailed upon to accept (as we both knew I would) his resignation.

He paid for lunch and we shook hands, expressing mutual regrets, going through the rituals of civilised behaviour, rituals which you deride when young but learn to see the utility of as you grow older. Because, when all else fails, it is to the outer forms that we cling, with the desperation of a drowning man.

• • •

I left work early; it was impossible to work that afternoon. Knowing that Jek was playing in a football game after class, I drove to his school on impulse and went to watch the game, in the long, encroaching shadow of the late afternoon sun. A flight of steps swept down from the assembly podium to the field; I sat on the top step, self-conscious and sweaty in my office clothes, remembering the football games of my schooldays, the way we would prolong them for hours, while the building emptied and grew silent, and the sound of the evening traffic cranked up, audibly, outside the school walls and that fierce, mid-afternoon glare gradually receded, without our knowing it, because we were reluctant to leave—unwilling that those wind-billowed afternoons of field, grass, sky, skidding falls, rushing ground, should end, stopping only when we could no longer see the hands of the clock on the neo-Victorian tower and knew it was time to go home.

Jek came pounding up the steps breathlessly.

"Dad, what are you doing here?"

"I thought I'd drive you home."

He gave me an odd look and said that a group of them were going out after the game.

"Tomorrow's a school day, isn't it?"

"Dad, don't be so *fustian*!"

I let him go. We always want to protect our young, beyond the time when they need protecting. And as I saw Jek's figure loping off the field, a glory of mud from head to ankle, I believed that nothing wrong, nothing untoward, would ever befall my son.

The Perpetual Immigrant

I have always wanted a daughter. Strange desire, for a Chinese. My mother grew up with the knowledge that she should have been left to die of exposure on a hillside in China at birth. Her parents already had three daughters; my grandfather's wrath was terrible. She was saved through the intervention of the midwife, who hid the baby in her house until my grandfather had simmered down somewhat. Grudgingly, he let the baby back into the family.

As if in recompense, my mother had three sons and I have four. But the sense of a narrow escape has haunted my mother all her life. At eighty, she shows no sign of flagging; a tiny, shrivelled doll in her *samfu*, jade bracelets clashing on her wrists, she sits on the sofa day after day, watching her imported Hong Kong soap operas. Her air of fragility is deceptive: her will to live is like a sacred flame tended by an acolyte—its intensity may vary, but it will never die. She saw my father to his grave and I think she may see me to mine.

• • •

I have been in this country for twenty-three years—more than half my life—but I never cease to feel like a stranger. Even now, I think of England as a mere stop-over on my journey, a blip on the perpetual immigrant's restless, shiftless trail for success. A country of narrow roads, narrow houses, narrow, grey vistas, and narrow, pursed lips saying, "Well, you should have thought of that sooner, shouldn't you?"—but of course I will never leave now. After all, for the perpetual immigrant, one place is very much like another. It is not an ideal country, but I am not a believer in Utopias. More importantly, I have my own restaurant—business concentrates the mind wonderfully—and whatever might be said about the English, they leave you alone if you leave them alone. In many ways the English and the Chinese are alike.

• • •

I forgot to mention that my two eldest sons are English. At least, their mother was English. The last time I saw her was five years ago, at a motorway restaurant of all places, on my way back to London from a business trip. She was in the company of a pale, red-haired, crumpled looking man. She hailed me across the length of the room: "Well, speak of the devil!" She wore a red leather jacket, white polyester pants, white sling-back high heels, pancake makeup—I noted all this, clinically—just like the hundreds, thousands, of women you see shopping at Sainsbury's or at the Co-op; I might have passed her without a second look in a crowded supermarket.

She seemed highly amused to see me. One of the things I had liked best and hated most about her was this cheerful, flippant irony, this refusal to fight. At the height of our worst quarrels, she had a habit of giving up; lighting up—she knew I hated the smell of cigarette smoke—she would blow smoke-rings and shrug, as if amazed that she had been induced to lose her temper. She thought I was terminally serious, woefully humourless and chronically bad-tempered. I expect she was right.

I thought of leaving the moment I saw her; only the thought that this would be unbearably rude and a sort of curiosity propelled me towards a table and fixed the neutral look on my face when she came over and insisted on sliding into the opposite seat. I had stopped hating her by then, but I still found it difficult to look directly at her.

She said she was glad we had met. I said I doubted that. "But I am," she said; she seemed hurt.

I told her I had my own restaurant now, and she smiled, absently. "Really? I always knew you would do all right."

I could see her reflection in the window pane. She had tried to keep her looks, what they call in the papers an English rose beauty, though the rose was turning a trifle brassy. Or perhaps I'm being uncharitable. The roots of her hair, as usual, were showing their natural dark brown; she had always been a little careless about keeping up the treatment. "I'll tell you a secret," I can still remember her saying, the first time we went out together; she looked at me, wickedly, checking to see whether I was breathless with anticipation, "I'm a *bottle blond*."

I asked her about her lover, the one she had run off

with after six years of marriage. She shrugged. "Oh, that soon blew over," she said, surprised that anyone could think it would last. "He was just an escape valve, nothing more." Yes, I imagine that the length and breadth of the country is littered with blown gaskets and shattered valves, relicts, reminders of her brief, tornado presence.

She seemed strangely nostalgic. "You're not still sore, are you?" she wanted to know. She meant, about her leaving. "It was all for the best, you know. It was an impossible marriage."

Before we had got married, she had warned me that she was impossible to live with. In fact, it was largely at my insistence that we shuffled down to the city registry one winter's day and became man and wife before a bored clerk, she grumbling all the while. Shacking-up had been out of the question: it would have prostrated my mother, who had visions of a grand wedding and a graceful, upward ascent into middle-class heaven. Actually, the whole rationale for my coming to England, in the first place, was to secure an education and I had wrecked my mother's shaky, but magnificent, edifice of dreams by falling for, as she inelegantly put it, the first floozy to walk down the street. Trust my mother to spot these nuances. She arrived from Hong Kong too late to stop the banns, as it were, and instead settled in, grimly, to keep the vigil of a deathwatch over my marriage. At least, that was what my wife said. As for my mother, she thought her daughter-in-law common. Years of living in a single-room flat in a decaying tenement in Kowloon had not altered her unshakable conviction one whit of her elevated station in life and the glory that was to come for me, her (hitherto) most promising son.

I am not sure what it means to be common. Perhaps it only means to be incapable of hypocrisy. My wife had told me, from the start, that she had had lovers and couldn't promise that she wouldn't have more. Two of her previous boyfriends had been black, a Jamaican and a Guyanese. She said she had a weakness for exotic men (including me). They say forewarned is forearmed, but in my experience that is almost never true.

I asked her whether she ever felt the need to see her children. She fiddled with the rings on her fingers.

"I always thought a clean break was better," she said, apologetically. Then she looked at me challengingly. "Anyway, I was never the maternal type. You knew that. It doesn't mean I don't think of them—what do they look like now?"

I said the younger one looked a lot like her. She laughed, pleased. "Well, let's hope they don't lead my life." Leaning forward, she touched my hand, lightly. I flinched, but she didn't notice. "What are you doing later?"

"Going back to London."

"If you like, we could meet later," she said, in all seriousness. "I know a hotel down the road..."

"What about your friend?"

"My friend?" She traced a circle on the table top and glanced back at him. He was drumming his fingers on the table, scowling.

"No thanks," I said. It would have hurt too much.

She studied me reflectively for a moment. "You always were a self-righteous Oriental bugger," she said without rancour. "How's my ex-mother-in-law? Still wrecking marriages for a living? I'm sorry, I shouldn't have said that, should I, I've broken about twenty codes of filial piety, haven't I? Oh dear. But seriously, look after the boys, will you? But of course you will." She gave her sudden, brilliant smile, tucked her hair back under her beret—a red one, which she wore cocked at an angle—and walked off, with that pert, jaunty step I had seen for the first time all those years ago in Liverpool. It was the mid-Sixties, I was barely a month off the plane, and the new city was throbbing with pop music, girls in incredibly short skirts and the heady infectiousness of being young. In the next few months people would be sporting metre-length hair and garish, primitive colours and designs. Ethnicity was in; Maoism was part of radical chic. I decided to cash in, who had never even looked at a girl before. "I've been told I'm a dead ringer for Marilyn," my future wife said to me, complacently. "Marilyn who?" "Why, Marilyn Monroe, of course, you big silly." I was twenty-three, she was twenty. I was homesick, bewildered and madly in love.

I never saw her again.

• • •

When they were young, the boys would ask me occasionally about Kay. James, the elder one, was six when she left, old enough to retain a tenacious memory of her. At dinner, he would make casual references to his mother: "Mum used to have a pair of dangling parrot earrings, didn't she? I saw a pair just like them in the shop today." And my mother would sigh and say, "What a terrible woman." And James would bang his fork on the table and go red in the face and start to shout, she was *not*, she was *not*, and I would have to send him to his room.

I think I have only spoken twice to the boys about their mother. Once to tell them that she was gone for a long holiday. Then, when even they began to notice that most people would have returned from a holiday by then, that she was not coming back. "You mean she's dead," James said, in his clear, ringing voice. I winced. I said, no, she wasn't dead, she simply wasn't coming back, that was all. I never spoke of her again; I had to get on with my curiously shrivelled life.

• • •

I might have spoilt James. Always precocious, he was the golden child of the household, the first-born, imperial god made flesh (I'm exaggerating). I skirted him carefully, hoping that in him my thwarted ambitions would be fulfilled.

At sixteen, though, came The Fall. Like a ripe fruit, James tumbled into The Socialist Workers' Party. He sported earrings in both ears, grew his hair long, and started bringing home white, long-limbed girls who draped themselves, fetchingly, over the furniture and said, brightly, "Oh, hello, Mr Chang," when I got back from the restaurant at two in the morning. Or, worse, tall underfed boys who clumped all over the house and played their mindless music at full volume. This louche behaviour maddened me. James and I had nightly rows, ridiculous arguments during which I yelled at him in Cantonese, and he, in English, lit into me for my ghetto mentality, my refusal to assimilate, my support for the *Conservative* Party, my God. Whereupon I told him that if he was ashamed of his heritage—at which quaint word he rolled his eyes—he could leave. Never darken my door again, etc.

Which he did, at seventeen. Walked out one day, into the sunset, to join a multi-racial repertory company, piously funded by a militantly left-wing local council, dragging its ideological baggage all over the country. We discovered later he does a skit on a Chinese restaurant owner whose English wife runs off with an insurance salesman. "Funny, poignant, moving," runs the blurb in the programme. Ha.

I admit I was stunned. My son, an actor. A left-wing stand-up comic trading on his ancestry for cheap laughs. For a time, I saw myself as a figure in a Thomas Hardyish novel of epic proportions, a man crippled and brought low by the cruel blows of fate and so on. (Now, I am simply resigned. Sardonic.) Prudently, James stayed away a year before revisiting the family home at Chinese New Year, to eat his way steadily through the festive spread, pocket the red packets, and depart trailing clouds of splendour.

I suppose, if nothing else, he has style; I will grudgingly say this for him.

Now that he no longer lives at home, we get along much better. He deigns to visit us every month or so, during which visits we continue the rough, joshing arguments that are a feature (the only feature) of our discourse.

He will say, "Dad, I just heard that in Oxford they're not letting four Chinese restaurateurs join the Conservative Party. Not quite one of us, old chap."

I will say, wearily, that it is important to be engaged in the political process, and that, in my opinion, the Conservative Party is simply the lesser of two evils. For a Chinese whose parents fled communism, the mincing routines of the Labour Party are like the dances of a wolf in sheep's clothing.

And James will say, "Lovely analogy, Dad. But you know what I think? It's like Groucho Marx, see. You know—I wouldn't join any club that would have *me*. The more the right tries to step on you with its policies on immigration and education, the more convinced you are they're right. It's a kind of psychological sadism. Getting flogged is the price of acceptance."

And, losing my temper, I will say, "If you're so smart, how come you're such a loser?"

And, grinning, he will skip into the room he used to share with his brother, and I will hear the sound of laughter and music.

• • •

We christened the younger boy Richard, but lately he has begun using his Chinese name. He calls himself Khy for short. I do not know how much of this has to do with the fact that his mother's name is Kay. He looks remarkably like her: he has her eyes, large, grey, always her most expressive feature, and he has her brilliant, unnerving smile. But unlike his mother and brother, he is quiet, a little reserved, with none of their facility for collaring attention the moment they walk into a room.

Unlike James, he has seldom given me any trouble. He helps out in the restaurant when he can, he does well at school. He knows I want him to go to university. At the moment his chief vice is skateboarding in a manic fashion around the neighbourhood and terrorising the old ladies. I see him often in the company of a tall American boy called Lou, the son of a writer, I understand, here to gather material for her next novel. Lou has a careless athletic rangeiness that the English boys lack, a long, tomahawk face affecting a stern, wary aloofness; he is always dressed entirely in black and has seven gold studs in his left ear. Once, going up to Khy's room, I found him lying face down on the bed, apparently fast asleep, while the American boy perched on the window sill, like a carrion bird, smoking and looking at Khy. Something in the way he was looking at my son made me tell him, sharply, that I did not allow smoking in the house. Amiably, he put out his cigarette. Another time—they were leaving the house—I saw Lou drape his arm around Khy's shoulders, draw him close and kiss him above the eye. Khy drew back and gave him a look of mildly rebuking surprise. They did not see me, I think.

The lives of one's children are such mysteries. Or perhaps it is better to keep one's knowledge within certain well-defined boundaries.

· · ·

My second wife is from Canton and I had never seen her before we got married. At least, I had seen a photograph of her, with her hair scraped back severely from her face, wearing a grave smile. By then, I was tired of living alone, tired of unsatisfactory one-night stands. The photograph showed no obvious deficiencies, and so I gave in to my mother's ceaseless importunings to find a wife. My mother's marriage was not happy—my father was a philanderer by profession—but the unhappily married always seem anxious to matchmake on behalf of the whole world. Delighted, my mother made all the necessary arrangements through the marriage bureau. It had been her idea to find me a foreign bride; she felt, I think, that someone with no ties in this country would be less given to bolt, would be self-shackled, to put it brutally.

Three months later, this unknown quantity—*my wife*—was duly deposited at Heathrow, speaking not a word of English. The customs officials somehow got it into their heads that, shy, stubborn and uncomprehending as she seemed, she had to be a drugs courier, and they kept her for hours. By then, I was furious at having to wait in the arrivals bay while the other passengers streamed past me, furious with myself for having yielded to my mother's schemes. But when she finally emerged, in tears, looking impossibly small and impossibly grateful to be met by me—the way she clutched at my hand, like a child homing in, instinctively, on the first trustworthy adult it sees—I knew, then, that whatever happened, this marriage would have to work. If only to save my face.

For she turned out to be much younger than I had been led to believe, nearer James' age, in fact, than mine. The boys looked at her, nonplussed. "Cradle-snatcher," James said in mock-horror. "*Child*-bride." It is a standard male fantasy—or so I am told—to marry someone half your age and twice as nubile, but her youth was an embarrassment to me. Still, here she was: one couldn't pack her off again like a defective TV set. We adjusted. She and I adjusted. I do not suppose it was easy for her, but she did not speak of it; she is the most silent and enigmatic woman of my acquaintance.

At first she seemed to me plain, her round, childish face contrasting oddly with the elderly floral dresses which were all she had brought with her. A dumpy, peasant woman, I remember thinking in the beginning, suitable only for bearing children and housekeeping. Mentally, I still kept comparing her to the other one, though I knew it was a self-defeating thing to do. A year after we were married, my second wife gave birth to twin sons, and we trooped, dutifully, to the hospital to view her lying, exhausted, in the cramped hospital bed, her duty done.

I seemed to detect a look of determination on her face never to be a victim again.

Back home, she resumed her daily routine, but there was a difference. The weight peeled off, like a skin waiting to be shed; her face now revealed a spare, angular, I won't say, beauty, but something arresting, a little disturbing, her high cheekbones arching through and touched with rouge. She wore a faint, cheap scent; her nails were painted a colour which, on a trip to Woolworth's, I found to be Fiery Magenta. I watched her like a hawk, with a silent fear; she was conscious of my scrutiny.

Once, she asked me, "Your English wife, where is she now?"

I said, "I don't know."

"She was a bad woman?" (She had been listening to my mother.)

"No," I said. "She was just different." And I said, half-jokingly, half-fearfully, "And you—maybe you will leave me too, one of these days."

"Who would I run to?" she said, simply, a little resentful at being classed, even potentially, with the 'bad one'. I left the room, before she could say (as I felt sure she was going to say) that she was grateful to me and knew her duty—two of the most depressing phrases that the Chinese like to use.

No, she will not leave, if only because of the twins. I have seen her crooning to them, with that fierce, possessive mother-love that the Chinese poets love to eulogise; there is something in the strong line of her back that

86

makes me think she would be prepared to lay down her life for them, these two black-haired, black-eyed babies sitting silkenly in their cots and shattering the night with their piercing cries. I had forgotten what it was like to have babies in the house—the smell, the noise, the sheer worry. She gets up, uncomplainingly, several times a night to tend to them; if I volunteer to help, she gives me that faint, resentful look, and I retreat.

Yes, she is a good mother, a good woman all round, I suppose, not in the least like the other one. After two years we have got used to each other and there is something companionable about our silences together. People sometimes ask me what it is like to enter into an arranged marriage in this day and age; their faces register polite incredulity. My answer is, I expected nothing, I am pragmatic, like all Chinese, and so I am content. Certainly, she will never fling a plate at my head or plunge me into a frenzy of jealousy, sending me out to scour the neighbouring pubs for her slender form and gurgling laugh before she takes her latest acquisition to bed. She will never put me through the humiliation of walking through massed ranks of Englishmen, propped against the bar, watching me, hearing my stuttered questions with amusement, and muttering, none too softly, about "Chinks on a bender." She has neat features, she stays at home, she looks after her sons. What more could a man want? Twice a day, I try to remind myself—it is all I ask for.

The Forerunner

My brother died, in the early hours of a Saturday morning, running, naked, arms outstretched, down the road into the path of an oncoming car. The car wasn't even going particularly fast. He died of concussion, later, on the way to hospital. He was seventeen. That made me the only son.

• • •

They did an autopsy on him and that was when they found the traces of drugs in his body. The pathologist called my mother to ask if she knew that her son was a dope-fiend. I can see my mother now, cradling the telephone between head and shoulder, her glasses perched on the top of her head and her eyes fixed in the middle distance, thinking of something else. "It could have been worse," she said. The pathologist hung up, disgusted. (Later, he included this anecdote in his best-selling memoirs.)

I knew what she was thinking of. She had just read a life of Marie Curie and she had told us about the part where Pierre Curie is in a road accident, trampled to death beneath a horse-drawn vehicle. For months, his wife kept the scraps of clothing smeared with the remnants of his brains, poor matted nerves, muscles and blood impressed onto threads. Recounting it, my mother went pale. My brother was unimpressed. "Ma, you're so morbid."

All the relatives came to the funeral, all the ones I knew and hated, and some new ones I had never seen before but knew I would hate. They came to gloat over my mother. First my father (who had committed suicide a few months before my brother's death), now my brother: surely, now, she would betray some signs of being human? She did not. She sat through the funeral service, straight, composed, wearing what I call her Buddha look, made up of double-lidded, veiled eyes, an intimation of hidden secrets, a preternatural calm. I have seen the same trans-fixed, unblinking expression on the faces of lizards. When I was little, she could quell me simply by directing that stare at me. She did not cry.

• • •

If my brother hadn't been my brother, I think I would have hated him.

Things came easily to him. Too easily. Exams, games, friends, my mother's wide-eyed, chiselled looks. He did everything well, but not too well; because of that, he could seem facile, a lightweight to some. "That daring young man on the flying trapeze," my mother called him once, satirically, and that was the family image of him—heedless, flyaway. "I don't know whom he takes after," my father used to say, meaning, my mother. I, on the other hand, take after my father. Even as a baby, I had a certain recognisable solidity.

• • •

And of course there were the girls. When I was eleven and he was fourteen, we made a pact. If I would screen his calls for him, he would lend me the pornographic magazines circulating like an underground river among the older boys in school. (The prefects ran the racket, their source being a fatherly bookseller in a second-hand bookshop in Bras Basah Road.) My mother could never be relied on to be either possessive or strict; she'd say, "Oh, hold on, dear," and my brother would be stuck for hours on end on the phone with some girl whom he couldn't remember but who claimed to have met him at the bus stop. Whole battalions of girls claimed to have met him at the bus stop. They fascinated me, these girls, with their long, silky fringes and belts pushed low over narrow hips, but I would never have dreamed of saying anything to them.

• • •

My brother was an insomniac. In his whole life, I had never known him to sleep more than four hours a night. Often, it was less. Dark shadows circled his eyes: he looked perpetually hung-over, prematurely dissipated, irresistibly seedy.

He'd be up half the night, prowling about the flat, making surreptitious calls to friends, smoking incessantly.

90

Sometimes he took long walks around the estate, sliding in at six in the morning, just in time for school. My mother never knew. She took a sleeping pill every night and went out like a light.

A few weeks before his death, my father, who'd magnanimously left home a year earlier when my mother said she couldn't stand to live with him any longer, came over and had a fight with my mother about this insomniac behaviour. According to my father, a friend of his had driven past the estate the night before and had seen my brother picking the lock of a car. And then, my father said dramatically, he *got* in and *drove* off.

My mother pondered this, and turned to my brother. "Is this true?"

"Of course not."

"Well," said my mother. "He's denied it. So what do you want me to do?"

She was always edgy when my father visited: guilt makes you fidgety, she said once, plants a tightly knotted coil of tension in you.

My father said it was clear that she was incapable of controlling the children and that he was going to sue for custody, my God, he was sick and tired of this. "Go ahead," my mother said. "Just go ahead." She was, is, a Catholic, though she never goes to Mass. She refused to divorce my father, who, still madly in love with her, agreed to a judicial separation for the sake of theological propriety. To everybody, this was yet another example of my mother's high-handed irrationality. My mother liked to say, wryly, that you could take a woman out of the Catholic church but you couldn't take the Catholic out of the woman.

My father called her implacable. Cold as ice. Hard as granite. My mother wore her faraway Buddha look, and I could understand my father's frustration. My mother and brother were elusive, evasive: when you thought you had them in the palm of your hand, they had already fled, with a swift, unthinking ruthlessness. My parents' marriage had always been a struggle, my father struggling to pin my mother down, my mother struggling to flee. Often, I had felt my mother's manic desperation, like that of an animal caught in a trap, willing to snap or chew a leg off in its single-minded desire to escape.

"Leave her alone," my brother said. My father hit him full across the face and he went down theatrically, like a ninepin. My mother snapped out of her gilded trance; I stood poised, ready to prevent a murder. Family life's better than Disneyland, my brother liked to say, there's never a dull moment. Magically, a red welt appeared across my brother's cheek.

"*Look* at him," said my father. "I mean, just *look* at him. He looks a mess. He's losing weight, he doesn't sleep, apparently. What sort of family is this, anyway?" To my brother, who was lying on the floor, staring at the ceiling and smiling beatifically: "Get up. You think this is some kind of game?"

"I've had enough of this," my mother said. She marched into the bedroom and locked the door.

My brother got up slowly, touching his cheek. "I think I'll wear this permanently. It's kind of cool. What do you think?"

My father sat down heavily, in the nearest chair. He looked old, defeated; for the first time I noticed that a whole new crop of white hairs had sprouted overnight on his head. "Promise me one thing," my father said. "Promise me you're not on drugs or anything stupid." He was a police superintendent in the narcotics unit. He was highly respected; he really was. It was only around his family that he wore the air of hurt bafflement that I'd come to associate with him.

"Dad," my brother said. "I got all A's in the exams, remember? Come on. This is stupid. But I promise." You could see why old ladies would unhesitatingly entrust him with the money they had so cunningly stuffed into their mattresses.

My father gave us both a hard stare. "It's not easy being a father."

"No," we said in unison.

He looked towards my mother's bedroom, wistfully.

"Sometimes she stays in there for a whole day," I said.

"Why are all of you conspiring against me?" my father said. "Why do I get pushed out of my own home and continue paying the bills? What did I ever do?" He was shouting by now.

"Nothing," my brother said. It was meant to be soothing, but it came out different—accusatory. And we all knew, more or less, that that was the trouble. In anybody

93

else's eyes, my father would have been the model parent and husband. But ordinariness, to my mother, in any shape, size or smell, was a death-knell. She would settle for nothing less than greatness. And it was no use expostulating, but who does she think she is? She didn't love him.

As he was about to go, he clapped my brother on the back. "So, tell me, did you really drive off in that car?"

"Dad, what do you take me for? One of those assholes you fuck about with during an interrogation?"

"*Watch* your language." He ruffled my hair (I hate that) and left.

• • •

Soon after this, my father killed himself.

They get confused in my mind sometimes, the two funerals. I have dreams where I'm not sure whom all the people in black are mourning, and my brother drifts past, asking, "Am I dead?"

Of course there are some details that belong exclusively to either occasion. Like the rows of policeman in uniform at the service for my father. They sat, perspiring stiffly in the heat, and afterwards they shook my mother's hand, one by one, carefully avoiding her eyes. They knew about my father's personal life and they knew whom to blame.

The thing I remember about my brother's funeral were the girls. Tall girls, short girls, mini-skirted girls, girls in long shredded skirts and feathery scarves, selfconsciously ethereal, hockey-playing girls with achingly sleek muscles. Skinny girls without figures, who huddled at the back of the church, hiding beneath their fringes, their long, slim legs tucked decorously under the seat, looking furtively around. "I didn't know he was a Catholic," they murmured. He wasn't. He was hedging his bets, or so he said.

All these girls were at the funeral. They all cried, silently, into handkerchiefs. As the cortege was leaving the church, one of them ran up to my mother, who was walking alone, a little ahead, and pressed something into her hand. It turned out to be a dried flower. She gazed at my mother directly, red-eyed. "He gave it to me," she said.

My mother turned on her the full, frightening serenity of her Buddha look. "Thank you, dear."

Outside the church, the girls held a heated discussion. Should they or should they not go with the family to the Columbarium?

Most of them elected to go. They were incandescent, alight with self-inflicted grief; they were proud of that grief, jealous of anyone who tried to wrest it away from them. Many had hardly known my brother and I thought it very peculiar that anyone would want to enter this charged, infected atmosphere of mourning for no good reason. I said, "Hi," to one of the girls, and she gave me a look of horror, as if I had indecently propositioned her or something. I wanted to tell her that it was possible to be anaesthetised by grief, that I'd had an excess of it in the past year. Years later, I imagined, they'd still be talking about this day, with nostalgia for the time when they could still love, purely and fiercely, from afar. My brother, the icon. My little groupies, he'd call them, lovingly.

• • •

Now and then I go to the Columbarium to put flowers in the little metal holder beside the stone tablets of my father and brother. It's a depressing place, I admit, miniature HDB grey blocks housing the ashes of the dead. My father and brother are placed side by side: my father's photograph shows him to be eternally forty-five, my brother is forever fourteen, gazing, wide-eyed and startled, at the camera. (After that, he refused to pose for photographs.) My mother never comes. I don't know why I do, unless it's a primitive suspicion that the dead are not really gone, that they need succour like everybody else.

• • •

The only girl who didn't go to the funeral was Rachel. She was sent to stay with relatives in Israel, or so I'd heard; she was supposed to purge her mind of all that had happened. I could see her at the beach, in some zebra-striped bikini and a pair of the blackest Africa shades, her little mouth set in a straight line. She would be outwardly demure and inwardly seething, plotting her escape.

When Rachel appeared on the scene, I knew she was different, somehow. She was quite mad, for one thing, and that appealed to my brother. Any streak of insanity appealed to him. He told me the story of Rachel on a combined schools camping trip. The instructor had fried a couple of slugs, to show how one could survive in the wild without provisions, and passed them around for consumption. No one, not even the boys, would touch them, except Rachel, who swallowed one unblinkingly.

I was quite keen to meet his slug-eating girl, but when I did, I was disappointed. She was small and slender, with a halo of hair surrounding an angelic, heart-shaped face; she looked terribly fragile, like somebody capable of breathing her last at any moment. When she smiled, her eyes narrowed and almost closed altogether, and her face wore an expression which I recognised from reproductions of the Mona Lisa. She was half-Jewish, half-Chinese, and had already been expelled from one school for disruptive behaviour. Without her parents' knowledge, she smoked a joint every morning for breakfast.

She was only two years older than I was, but the gap seemed vast, unbridgeable. "Hello, kiddywinks," she'd say when she saw me, and I'd go red all over. I didn't like her. She was dangerous.

The first time they made me try the stuff, nothing happened. Or rather, nothing seemed to happen. The three of us were sitting on the sofa, the two of them watching me benevolently, my brother's fingers entwined in Rachel's hair. "This is boring," I said. "You have to go with the flow," my brother said. They were both free falling, floating, moving in lunar time. I tried to get up to go to my room, and found I couldn't move. My legs wouldn't move. I broke out in a cold sweat; sweat was pouring off the bridge of my nose. "Hey, you guys," I said. And then I was sick all over. I was sick for the rest of the night.

"The stuff was too strong, I guess," my brother said, sorrowfully, after helping me to the bathroom for the fifth time and holding my head over the toilet bowl. But I knew that wasn't the real reason. I was meant for the straight and narrow. I had no wish to expand my horizons or climb onto higher planes of consciousness. I relished normality. It was just that, in my family, normality had been scuppered in its infancy.

• • •

So anyway, there was Rachel and there was my brother and there didn't seem to be any room for me in between. I watched them together, and I knew they thought they were the favoured ones, the ones who could glide through barriers and emerge on the other side, intact, more alive. "They'll learn," said my mother, who viewed all my brother's amorous escapades with detachment.

Rachel's family was exotic by our standards, "sickeningly liberal," she called them once. Her Jewish grandparents had fled the anti-Jewish upheavals in Baghdad after the Second World War. An uncle on her Chinese mother's side was a CPM guerilla. All this had bred in her parents a dour insistence on the importance of liberty and freedom of the individual. Dinner table discussions centred, relentlessly, on politics and the human condition in general; her father dabbled in human rights activism and more than once nondescript men had come to take him away for questioning. Rachel was the youngest of four children, the unexpected product of her parents' middle age—for her, they had always been elderly, embroiled in dead, antiquarian struggles.

"I believe in the three A's," Rachel said. "I'm amoral, apathetic, apolitical. I'm in the vanguard of the new youth."

All this meant nothing to me. When I looked at Rachel, I saw someone capable of walking on burning coals, who probably ate shards of broken glass for breakfast, with her inimitable jaunty air. She was destroying my brother.

"Destroying, piffle," she said. She was waiting for my brother at the corner of our block of flats, when I returned from school that day. I had never heard anyone say "piffle" before.

"He doesn't sleep any more," I said. "Not since he met you." Not since he started smoking pot and taking pills to help him relax through the night. He blanked out, drifted off, which was what he wanted. But in the morning he was more wrecked than ever. He was no longer pretend-seedy. He was genuinely seedy.

"You really admire him, don't you?" Rachel said. "It's quite touching, in a way."

"Why don't you leave him alone?"

"Please," Rachel said. "Please don't make him out to be some pathetic victim or whatever. He knows what he's doing." I stared at her and began to walk off. "It's just that he doesn't want to be ordinary," she explained to my back. "He wants to be extraordinary." She was *that* far gone.

• • •

Like some nocturnal creature, my brother only really came into his own at night. At night, his eyes lit up like 100-watt light bulbs and he was running about the flat in a passable imitation of those mice you see in pet shops, going round eternally on the toy wheels in their cages, expending energy uselessly, frantically. He was so febrile he looked as if his hair might catch fire of its own volition.

I couldn't sleep either. I had never seen him like this before and I was worried. I hovered around, scared he'd take a nose-dive from an open window (my mother had never got around to fixing metal grilles) and end up splattered all over the pavement; everybody loves a tragedy, as long as it happens to somebody else. The drugs did things to my brother: I saw him depressed, hysterical, ecstatic. But what really put me into a blue funk was his thinking he could fly. "I can fly," he'd say, looking straight into my eyes, and I'd look away, for fear of being mesmerised into believing him, he was so convincing. And he was forever dangling out of the damned windows.

I'm counting the lights in the block of flats opposite, my brother would call to me at night, dreamily. During the day, it looks drab, grey, and utilitarian, but at night this gigantic checkerboard takes on a symbolic, magical quality. It's a swarming warren of secrets, and I can decipher them, if I want to. Daylight is the spell destroyer. It picks out the cracks in the walls, it lays an accusing finger over the whole blighted landscape. I like the night, little brother.

• • •

I couldn't watch him all the time. Sometimes I nodded off, and then it was my brother who made breakfast, turned on the bathroom heater and got us both ready for classes. He'd be exhausted, but cheerful. All perfectly normal. Except that he would swallow a couple of brightly coloured pills with his coffee and, when he reached the bus stop, he was as high as the stratosphere, beatified, tanked up with gallons of euphoria to get him through the day.

When I was little, and prone to getting beaten up by the school bullies, I used to tell my brother I wished I was him, liked by everybody. "Don't ever wish to be me," he said. "Where's your self-esteem?" He got quite fierce. "Don't ever wish to be me."

• • •

The names were like an incantation. Downers, uppers, speed, Quaaludes, amphetamines, Benzedrine, acid, valium. (My mother took the valium.) Poetry. I liked the names.

• • •

We had a fight one night. "You're a junkie," I screamed at him, though, technically, I knew you had to be doing heroin to qualify as one. Lately, I'd started looking out for hypodermic needles—I hadn't found any in the flat yet, but I was far from complacent. Pills were already beginning to infest my dreams: they whirled, in gaudy-coloured arabesques, through my sleep.

My brother cocked an eyebrow, and wandered about, whistling.

• • •

His grades were slipping, of course, and he was dropped from the school tennis team, because his game was falling apart. But it wasn't the sort of thing that rang alarm bells: people put it down to our father's death, girlfriend trouble, the flu, whatever. Nobody would have believed me if I'd told the truth. Not my *brother*.

Rachel's father was a pharmacist; he was her unwitting supplier. She'd go down, after school, and have the run of the place, under the pretence of helping Daddy in his work. Rachel had the cool methodical efficiency of a genius, never creaming too many pills at any one time and never too many of the same. Her strength lay in her capacity for self-restraint, which sounds an odd thing to say, but it was true—she never once slipped up in her accounting methods, she never once went overboard. What she hated most in the world were crazed druggie types—no, what she was after was a managed detachment from reality. It wasn't her fault that it was my brother who betrayed her in the end, with his self-destructive messiness; he was her one conspicuous failure. Anyway, she looked so sweet, and serious, she had eyes like Bambi's, and hair like a sun-spattered cloud, who would've suspected her? Certainly not her father.

She caught my brother once with another girl, holding hands and strolling around a shopping centre. She watched from afar, wearing that ineffable Mona Lisa smile. The next day, she tracked the girl down, grabbed her by the wrist and twisted it hard; the girl gave a muffled scream. Rachel never stopped smiling. "You leave him alone," she said gently. For someone so tiny, she was very strong, and no one ever doubted she meant what she said. She was convinced that she and my brother had a destiny together; she was oracular about this, and mean as hell.

I thought a lot about what to do. My mother, I knew, was hopeless, locked tight in her own remote Lapland of the mind. My father was dead. The day before my brother's death, I called the pharmacy where Rachel's father worked. "Mr Abraham," I said. "You don't know me, but I had to make this call." "What?" "Why don't you check the stores after Rachel's been through them?" "Who is this?" Seized by fright, I hung up. But by then, it was too late.

• • •

Picture this.

Picture a party at the flat, my brother and his friends, to celebrate the start of the holidays. I haven't asked any of my friends: they are only thirteen-year-olds and I don't want them to be laughed at. By now, in any case, I have become a twenty-four-hour self-appointed guardian angel for my brother, and this unceasing vigilance doesn't leave me time for anything else.

Midnight. Most of the food is plundered and gone, or scrunched underfoot. The point of these parties is not to eat, anyway. It is to look and be seen and to make out. The sitting room is cleared of furniture, and someone is performing a complicated dance routine. Everybody claps. The music is loud, hypnotic, high-frequency; I imagine bats in remote parts of the island pricking up their ears, receiving the message. Someone has brought vodka and it is passed around, sacramentally. So as not to look out of it, I drink a glassful. It is colourless and tasteless, and I feel fine. My mother would not approve, but my mother is in Malaysia, visiting relatives. Out of the corner of my eye, at the knife-edge of my vision, I see Rachel threading her way in and out of the crowd, an evil, little elf in a tight, body-hugging, gold-patterned number. She is bite-sized and delectable, and moves with a confident, loose-jointed swing. Leaning against my brother, she barely comes up to his shoulder. He puts his arms around her and squeezes her tight; she laughs and pummels him, and he bites her ear, smiling.

I don't know who makes the suggestion to play strip-poker. The girls dissent, groaning. Rachel pops a pill into her mouth and slips one to my brother. It could be candy, for all I know. It's late and the excitement is growing, an excitement born of the hour and the heady vodka fumes, a boisterousness tinged, unspoken, with sex. Most of the girls leave, squeamishly, en masse—they are nice girls, and this sort of thing, on top of the vodka, is beyond them. A couple of boys gallantly offer to escort them home. I can imagine the rumours the next day.

Rachel stays, offering to play. "No," says my brother. "Yes," she says, glaring at him, and he has nothing more to say.

The rules are, footwear and accessories first, accessories being watches, bracelets, earrings, necklaces, scarves, caps, followed by the rest of one's clothes. The idea is to prolong the titillation as far as possible. My brother changes the music; no more House, instead The Doors come on, with *The End*, sepulchral, camp, ludicrous. "Yeucch," someone says, but by then they're far too engrossed in their game to notice. Things have got to the stage where a joint is being passed round and people are dragging on it, without really knowing what they are doing. They are all decent, middle-class kids, whose idea of depravity is to smoke a cigarette. They have no idea how far my brother has transgressed their unwritten boundaries.

My brother is losing, badly. He is down to his jeans and he is lying on his stomach on the floor, his bare feet thrust ceilingwards. He is too toked up to concentrate and he makes bad guesses, wild guesses. I think he wants to lose. I sit on the bed, watching the game; I haven't been asked to play. Rachel, on the other hand, sits demurely, her legs curled beneath her, her cards held high, primly, so no one can see them. Now and then my brother makes mock grabs at her cards and she swats him hard, with her fists, like a street-brawler. I can feel the exhilaration coming off my brother in waves of psychic energy: he is in love with the world, with humanity, but especially with Rachel.

Now The Doors are playing *Light My Fire*, and everybody has lost at least a shoe, except Rachel. The weed is beginning to take effect and everybody is shiny with perspiration: they think they're acting normally, but to me it's obvious that everyone is operating in a time-frame of his own and is puzzled why the others all seem to be too slow, or too fast, in their motions. It's funny, like a film where the sound and the action have ceased to synchronise. But it's a good feeling building up, a feeling that one can live forever.

My brother disappears into the kitchen to get more ice, and Rachel follows him. They are gone for a long time, and I'm sent to see what's happening. What's happening is that they're necking by the sink: Rachel's small hands have burrowed inside my brother's jeans and he is busy unzipping her dress. They move apart, unhurriedly, when they see me. "Hello, kiddywinks," Rachel says.

"Shut up," I say.

"Don't be rude," my brother says, smacking me. I hit him back and for a moment we glare at each other, heaving. I know, despite the fact I'm younger, that I can defeat him now in any fight; he has lost so much weight in the past few weeks that he's almost emaciated, the ribs in his chest are sticking out.

"Stop it," Rachel says, and places herself between us. My brother's arms encircle her waist. She is always between us.

The others are hollering for the game to continue. "Let's get rid of them," my brother says to Rachel. She nods, and slips him another pill, from her purse. He gulps it down with a glass of water.

I go and lie down on my bed. The vodka has gone to my head and I feel as if I'm being attacked by a sledge-hammer. I'm tired of this party, though I like the jangling, demented guitars on *Light My Fire*, which my brother is playing again, defiantly. It sounds out of tune and yet in tune, pointless and yet full of cosmic meaning. This is the closest that my brother and I have come to a punch-up in a long time. I turn on my side and in a moment I'm asleep. In the one wasted minute I take my eye off my brother, he gets himself killed.

• • •

By this time, the brakes are off: in my brother's mind, he has circled the globe and back again, and is heading, feverishly, towards intergalactica. Everybody else is just so slow, winning, losing, playing, talking. All his life, he has been waiting for others to catch up with him. He wants, needs, to speed things up. By then his jeans have been dragged off, with much screaming ribaldry and sly glances at Rachel. My brother lopes about the room in bright red underpants, ignoring the protests of the others that he's trying to look at their cards. He leans out of the window, giving them his usual post-midnight rendition of how he can decipher the secrets of the night; they have to haul him back, bodily, from the window.

"I'll raise you," my brother says to Rachel. His cards are a mismatched motley. She shows her hand; she has four aces. My brother lets out a whoop; Rachel rolls her eyes. And before the others know what is happening, he has streaked out of the door, and down the stairs to the ground floor. They pelt after him in a rush, getting entangled in the doorway; laughing, out of breath, they glimpse him running, naked, ahead of them, straight across the grassy verge that marks the boundary of the estate, and hurtling into the road.

• • •

They stand at the top of the grass slope, staring at the body sprawled on the road. It looks white, unevenly marbled, under the light of the fluorescent street lamps. The driver of the car stands on the pavement, shaking his head and flailing his arms in stupefaction. He starts to shout: Why couldn't the stupid kid watch where he was going?

One by one, they step out of the dark and surround my brother, jostling for view. They are awed. This is the first person their age they know personally who has died. They wish, fleetingly, that it had been a more sublime death: this smacks of the faintly ridiculous. Still in this, as in everything else, my brother is the forerunner: they have yet to achieve non-existence. Someone whimpers. There is no blood. He lies very still, face-down.

They will remember this, and mythologise it.

• • •

Hours after they had taken the body away, Rachel was still sitting at the top of the grassy slope, clasping her knees. She was so rigid she seemed frozen. Nobody could get her to move and, in the end, they left her there, after calling her parents. I found her crouched, kneading her fingers into her palm. There didn't seem to be anything to say. We sat for hours, it seemed, without talking. Then her parents drew up in their car, and she was off and running towards the road, with some mad idea of flinging herself in front of another vehicle—I don't know—except that her father cornered her and dragged her back, she twisting and turning all the while, and that was the last I ever saw of her.

• • •

I don't hate her any more. I wish I did. At least you know you're alive when you hate someone.

Contingencies

He knows Kok Cheong, in a desultory fashion, from school: it is assumed that they are friends, since Kok Cheong says so. The truth is that Tom's primary emotion towards Kok Cheong has always been one of tepid indifference, though he has never had the heart to tell Kok Cheong, who has, over the years, taken his fealty for granted. Tom had drifted through school in a pleasant haze; his reports had always said, "has the intelligence, but won't make the effort." Kok Cheong, on the other hand, had been one of the golden boys, top student, fleet athlete, school prefect. Tom has always hated the guts of these golden boys, with a cordial, visceral hatred. But he has noticed that they frequently choose as friends someone less bright, less popular, grateful for whatever scraps of reflected glory are available. He knows that Kok Cheong has selected him for the role of sidekick, court jester; he ought to mind, but somehow he doesn't. In any case, he sees little of Kok Cheong these days, now that he is studying medicine at the university, and Tom is in business administration, fitfully trying to muster an interest in the details of business while his mind wanders into riffs, licks, snatches of Muddy Waters songs. He plays blues guitar in a pub at weekends, and he would play full-time if he could, except that his parents would have a fit if he failed to get his degree. (Tom is nothing if not filial.)

Occasionally, he sees Kok Cheong cruising around campus in a shiny black convertible sports car, which elicits untold envy in the mind of every right-thinking male student. Kok Cheong's father is a heart specialist with a lucrative practice. Tom's father is a primary schoolteacher with a homicidal dislike of eleven-year-olds.

Lately, the buzz around campus is that Kok Cheong is going out with a girl called Christie. Tom has seen her around, a tall, long-legged girl with a mass of kinked hair that changes colour every month. She is supposed to be Filipino, Eurasian, he is not sure. She is well-known for wearing red bustiers to class, causing the more faint-hearted tutors to wilt, and for her string of boyfriends, all of whom are uniformly wealthy and, strangely, quite dull. Kok Cheong is wealthy, but rather less dull: he does, after all, have a black sports car and a fondness for baggy Italian clothes which do hang rather well on his athlete's body, admittedly. Soon, Kok Cheong, Christie and the black sports car are a combined fixture in the leafy lanes of Kent Ridge.

• • •

Soon after this, he runs into them at the pub where he plays on weekends. Cornered by Kok Cheong during an intermission, he is dragged, unwillingly, to where Christie is sitting by the car. She extends a slim hand.

"I like your bracelet," Tom says, for want of something to say.

With a swift, unthinking movement, she holds her wrist up to the light. The bracelet is composed of human teeth. "Oh, wow," he says. Now he really doesn't know what to say.

"I used to go out with a dentist," she says.

He senses that she is gently poking fun at him, and he decides to ignore her. Up close, he thinks her rather plain, even gawky; all her features seem a little too large for her face, and she is too thin and bony. She is smoking steadily, sunk into herself; her right foot taps with a sort of suppressed energy on the floor.

"She collects body parts," Kok Cheong says, and there is something in his voice which makes Tom look at him. Yes, the signs are unmistakable: the guy is moony, possessive, proprietary and quite ridiculously happy. He is in the mood where everything and everybody seem good, kind and explicable to him, and he wants to share this feeling. Tom, conscious of a rising irritation, excuses himself.

Back on stage, he is acutely conscious of Christie's presence, without actually looking at her. He knows she is still smoking; he sees again the way she drags on a cigarette, with that tender, defensive flick of the wrist; he senses her looking over the heads of the crowd, in her distant manner. He thought her silly and negligible; he is wrong.

• • •

When his set finishes, they are still hanging around by the bar. Kok Cheong has seized him again and is suggesting they go to the beach. Tom says he wants to go back and sleep. "Sleep is for the dead," Kok Cheong says. Tom shrugs. Don't they want to be alone? But a lack of anything better to do, some instinct of curiosity, makes him agree.

They pile into the black sports car, Kok Cheong and Christie in front, he at the back with his guitar, which goes with him everywhere. Kok Cheong is a little drunk and drives erratically; Christie sometimes grabs the wheel, and Tom expects the police to appear at any moment and to ask them to pull over. Still, he likes the feeling of the wind ripping past and shredding the sound of the music from the radio. He studies the back of Christie's head, thoughtfully.

They make it to Changi intact and stumble out of the car. A sudden silence is ringing in Tom's ears, after the roar of the wind. He is amazed by the amount of activity still going on at the beach: barbecues in their last throes, people sitting on mats listening to radios. Now and then an incoming aeroplane roars overhead, so near that he can make out the shape of the wheels protruding as the plane, a gawky bird, prepares to land. There was a time when the idea of an all-night vigil in itself used to excite him, but those days are past: it has been ages since he saw the sun rise.

They move further down the beach, to where it is darker and more secluded. Now they are stumbling over couples lying treacherously in unseen sandy hollows and beneath clumps of bushes; an angry murmuring begins to make itself felt underfoot, like the rumbles of an unseen giant coming to life. Christie is beginning to burst with suppressed laughter; taking off her shoes, she runs on ahead, pealing. Then she starts skimming stones across the surface of the water. The shadows of disgruntled couples can be seen retreating further down the beach.

Kok Cheong says, out of Christie's earshot, "We just got engaged today."

"Yeah?" Tom is surprised. Then, remembering his manners, "Congratulations."

"What? Oh, yes. Of course we can't get married for years yet. Not until I've started practicing."

"Well, if it's what you want."

"It is, it is." Kok Cheong is kicking at the sand, absently. "At least, I think so. It just sort of happened."

"You don't have to justify yourself."

"I guess not," Kok Cheong says, drily, and then he is grabbing Christie round the waist and they are scuffling, like unruly puppies. Tom flops on his back, and stares at the night sky. It is full of stars, and he wishes he knew their names, but he doesn't. He has never managed to identify the constellations on his own and he doesn't think he ever will; anyway, he likes them as random clusters, just as they are.

• • •

It is four A.M. on Sunday morning, but they won't hear of letting him go. Kok Cheong insists that they all go to his house for coffee. Kok Cheong, especially, is kind and solicitous towards Tom, while Tom, for his part, is succumbing to a deplorable savagery. He knows this smug self-absorption of fresh couples, their need to have an ordinary mortal around as a touchstone by which they can gauge their own radiance and reassure themselves that, yes, they are lucky.

Tom has been to Kok Cheong's house before, on a similar occasion, except that at that time the girl was a model called Janina, and Tom hadn't liked her at all. Light-headed with lack of sleep, he notes that Kok Cheong's house, which is a gruesome pastiche of a Southern plantation owner's homestead, has acquired a second set of gates. Both gates are electronically operated and swing open in an impressive, squeak-free silence. Both are made of shatterproof glass, with a crystalline sunburst emblazoned in the middle. Would two gates keep out burglars better? He shelves this interesting question, momentarily.

"I heard you got engaged," he says to Christie, when Kok Cheong has disappeared into the kitchen to look for food.

"We were drunk," she says.

"Well, congratulations on having got engaged while drunk."

"Don't be sarcastic."

"I'm not. I'm trying to say the conventional thing."

"Well, don't," she says, frowning. She takes out another cigarette.

"Why do you smoke so much?"

"Why do you ask so many questions?"

He throws up his hands.

"You don't like me, do you?"

It is on the tip of his tongue to say she is wrong, but he doesn't.

"I'll show you something," she says, abruptly.

They go out to the garden, down some steps into a sort of sunken grotto. Leaves brush against his face, like webbing; he smells the cloyingly sweet, overpowering smell of frangipani, and bumps, unawares, against metal bars. Then he sees them, about a dozen white cockatoos, asleep on their perches in an aviary taller than he is. They look like carved, feathered statues, snowy white in the darkness.

"They cost a fortune," Christie says, "and they're as noisy as hell."

As if on cue, the birds awake; seeing the two intruders, they range themselves against the bars of their cage in an impotent fury, screeching with all the shattering intensity of a siren breaking the silence of the night; the din is amazing. He and Christie run for the house, pulling the front door shut; the screeching subsides to a distant crackle.

Christie is laughing. "The last batch of cockatoos they had," she is saying, "someone set them loose in the middle of the night. You can see them flying about wild, in the neighbourhood. I think that's why the ones in the cage are so furious—they can hear the other cockatoos, the free ones, mocking them."

An apocryphal story, he thinks later; then, he is struck by the proprietary air with which she recounts it, the air of a chatelaine showing a guest around. She would like to be the owner of this gruesome Southern plantation pastiche; she likes, he hazards, money.

"I hate birds," he says. Ever since he saw the Hitchcock film, as a matter of fact.

Lying on the sofa, she lights up one of her inevitable cigarettes. Her movements have a rangy carelessness as she blows smoke rings, very deliberately, at the ceiling. "Why don't you sit down?" she says; she is mocking him.

Kok Cheong comes back in with coffee. "We saw your pets," Tom says.

Kok Cheong rolls his eyes. "My father. His obsession. Once he got two parrots and was trying to teach them the National Anthem but they never got past the Majulah. Now he's moving onto guinea pigs and hamsters." He slips onto the floor, wraps his arms casually around Christie's long legs. "He keeps two of them in a cage beside his bed. He calls them Laurel and Hardy. When Mum isn't around, he slips them into the bed—"

Christie laughs.

"—and lets them twinkle over his stomach. Oh, hi, Mum."

Kok Cheong's mother is tiny, but lethal; the most impressive thing about her is her punk haircut, which stands up in waving anemone tendrils a half inch or so from her scalp; she is also clad in a kimono dressing gown with pink dragons imprinted on it. A fifty-year-old doctor's wife with a rock sensibility; Tom warms to her. She is, he knows, the owner of a string of very successful boutiques. Eccentricity, apparently, is not a bar to the accumulation of wealth in this family.

"Hello, Tom," she says. To Kok Cheong, "Have you been defaming your father again?" She nods, coolly, at Christie, while Kok Cheong unwraps his fiancée and does a fair impression of twiddling his thumbs. He is in awe of his mother; she was the one who bought the black sports car for him, after all.

"So what's happened to Janina?" she asks Kok Cheong, pleasantly.

"Over," he mutters, sulkily. "Over." As if in answer to an unbidden signal, he follows his mother into the kitchen.

"She hates me," Christie says, stating a fact. Tom nods; the mothers of sons always hate girls like Christie—it seems to be a universal law. She adds, dreamily, "I hope I have daughters later on. If I have a son, I'm going to leave him on the hillside to the elements. An ancient Chinese tradition." Seeing his face, she says, kindly, "I'm just joking, lah." But he senses that she means it.

That night, Tom dreams of cockatoos in flight through the trees in a white blur of anger.

• • •

Tom's band is called The Leopards. A dreadful name, coined largely because the lead singer, Hamzah, used to like to wear leopard-spotted trousers of a life-threatening tightness; now they are stuck with it, even though Hamzah has since discovered B.B. King and Otis Redding and John Lee Hooker and now wears torn jeans with army boots, the street-cred-prole look. Built like an American football player, he can do a high, mincing falsetto and a sexy James Brown growl.

The last band member is Animal (actually Anun Chandran), but he has been known as Animal for as long as anyone can remember. Very thin and hirsute, he is popularly supposed to change into a werewolf when there is a full moon. Animal plays the drums. He once studied law, but it gave him such nightmares he soon threw it up. On stage, he has been known to throw the drum sticks at the audience in his exuberance and to continue walloping the drums with his bare hands.

Tom is the quiet workhorse of the band; he prefers it that way.

They have come to an accommodation with the management. For every hard blues number they play, they have to do what the management calls "crowd pleasers." The management has definite ideas about crowd pleasers. These include, *A Horse With No Name*, *Speedy Gonzalez*, *I Just Called To Say I Loved You* and *Hello*. Among The Leopards, this is known as the List of Increasing Pukability, but it's either that or not playing at all. The Leopards are pragmatic.

"We'll be back," Hamzah promises the audience, "in half an hour." Scattered applause; most people are too busy roaring at two television screens propped over the bar, playing reruns of *I Love Lucy*.

Unstrapping his guitar, Tom sees Christie for the first time, sitting alone in a corner. She is looking directly across at him. It has been a week since he last saw her at Kok Cheong's house, and he hasn't been able to stop thinking about her. Her smile comes swimming at him out of dreams, like a Cheshire cat's; he finds himself mentally composing songs around the motif Christie; he wonders, distractedly, where it will all end.

He makes his way across and squeezes in beside her. Her hair has a light reddish tinge this week and is done up in a knot just below her neck. It is too difficult to talk above the din emanating from the speakers, so he orders two Cokes, and they sit in a companionable silence, waiting for his next set.

• • •

Backstage, Animal, who sees everything (like God), wants to know what Christie does.

"She's studying Economics at the university."

"Good grief," Animal says in horror.

• • •

Tom has no illusions about his looks. He is not good-looking, not in the conventional sense. Residual acne scars have given his face a craggy, weathered texture; he could be taller; his hair is thick and wiry and he keeps it cropped short, military-style, to prevent it from sprouting into an Afro aureole. On the other hand, years of swimming for his school have given him a good build and he does have nice eyelashes, as his aunts keep telling him, impervious to his embarrassment.

Tom is the youngest in his family. His two elder sisters have long since married and moved out; they visit on weekends, swooping down in a flurry of rackety children, morose husbands and a level of noise and bustle which seems inordinate but necessary, though Tom can't fathom why. His sisters, used to seeing him as the baby, pull his hair, tug his clothes and inquire with meaningful winks after his girlfriends, especially a girl called Li-Shen whom he used to date in his teens and was rash enough to introduce to his devouring family. She is now in the United States doing computer science and Tom can't even remember what she looks like, though she still writes to him regularly. In answer to his sister's queries, he says he intends to stay celibate.

"Please don't bother him about girls!" Tom's mother always cries, at this juncture. She is the antithesis of Kok Cheong's mother, a housewife who wears faded floral prints long after they have ceased to be fashionable and is letting her hair, heavy with pins, go grey; a gifted cook, her happiest moments are spent swapping recipes with her daughters. She is not happy about Tom playing in a band, but sees it as an aberration, something wayward and adolescent that will stop once he graduates, finds a job and loses his soul. A kindly, fussy woman who worries too much, she sees hidden traps and temptations for Tom everywhere: chief on her list of vices is Woman, followed closely by music.

Tom's father is a well of silence in this commotion prone family. Years of hectoring primary school pupils during the day have left him voiceless, averse to talk, at night. At night, he reads thick volumes of history in his room, all the wars, depredations and political ineptitudes throughout the ages. Reading history has made him dry and cynical: he believes firmly that all politicians should be shot.

Tom is the first member of his family to go to university. Because of that, he knows, he is treated with a sort of totemic reverence which irritates him, and frightens him, too: he is expected to bring home the goods.

• • •

Lying in bed, his radio turned low to Billie Holliday, Tom cannot sleep. The murmuring silence around him nudges him awake, every time he is on the verge of dropping off; as only true insomniacs know, the dead of night is the noisiest time of all. He tries counting sheep, tries counting the number of cars grazing past way below at the foot of his block of flats, but nothing works. He picks up the phone and dials Christie's number.

"Hmm?" she says into the phone, a sleepy cat's murmur; then "Tom?"

"Did I wake you?" he says, knowing it is a stupid question.

Long silence; he is afraid she will hang up, and he knows that sharp, definitive click of the receiver will finish him off forever. "No-o," she says at last. "I was waiting to be woken up. Talk to me, Tom." She came to him, he reminds himself, all gold and smoke-wreathed and confident.

So he talks to her about the first thing that comes into his head, the blues and how he discovered it, and his heroes and his burning, inchoate desire to escape, knowing he sounds like a fool and not caring, all through the long, slow slide to dawn.

• • •

The next time, it is she who calls him. He leaps for the phone, afraid his mother will reach, martyred, for it, and hear Christie's voice. The phone is in the hallway; he lies on the floor on a cushion, legs propped over the back of a chair, hand cupped over the receiver to muffle the sound of his voice. Living on the fourteenth storey, the only shadows cast on the walls of his living room are the humpbacked shadows of passing clouds. For the first time in years, he watches the sun rise.

• • •

They play twenty questions. Christie won't talk about herself; usually the most she will answer to a question is yes or no.

"What school did you go to?"

"A convent."

"Which one?"

"That's a secret."

"What did you like best about school?"

"Roller-skating. I used to go early every morning and skate like mad in the basketball court, round and round. I wanted to be a speed skater. Until one morning, I crashed into a wall bordering the court and broke my nose. I was in hospital for a week. After that Sister—Sister Mary—banned all roller-skating in school. I was so upset I cried."

He imagines her lying back in bed, amidst a welter of pillows and cushions, twirling a chain on her index finger.

"Do you love him?" he asks, abruptly, too abruptly.

"Who is *he*? she asks, innocently.

"Do you believe in love?"

A long pause. "Tom, you're getting sentimental," she says, and puts the phone down. The nightly teasing ritual is over.

• • •

"I paid a thousand dollars for the engagement ring," Kok Cheong says. "And I still haven't told my parents about us."

Kok Cheong's voice over the phone sounds very much the same as it does in person, low, precise, every word clearly articulated, authoritative, even when he is confessing to doubts. Tom, cradling the phone on his shoulder, draws tiny guitars on a memo pad. He wants to get off the line, but cannot bring himself to be dismissive. He has always found it difficult to shatter the images which other people have of him, and Kok Cheong's is particularly inviting. Tom knows he is seen as trustworthy, loyal: it has something to do with the deceptively open face he bears, a look which mothers and old ladies gravitate towards, instinctively. It has made him the repository of more secrets than he cares to remember. He cannot help having the sort of face he has.

Kok Cheong has been calling Tom, on the flimsiest excuses, which are merely pretexts to talk about Christie. A note of dissatisfaction has infiltrated his happiness; he has begun counting the flies in the ointment. He starts with the most trivial. He doesn't like the way Christie smokes all the time; it gives her nicotine-stained nails; kissing her is like kissing an ashtray. At this, Tom laughs out loud, while a tiny, internal polyp of hate grows at the thought of Kok Cheong and Christie, together.

Kok Cheong registers the laugh, grimly, and continues his litany. "I don't know," he says. "I think about her all the time; I try not to think about her all the time. I asked her what she wants, and she says she wants us to be together, the next minute she says, no, she doesn't want that at all, so I ask her, does she want to break off the engagement? And she says, yes, then no, then your mother doesn't like me, which is true, but that's never bothered Christie before. OK, that's bad enough, but she's got these mood swings, you know, first she's laughing, then she gets all furious and won't talk to me, then she gets hysterical and wants to fly a kite at East Coast at eleven at night, and this is driving me crazy, you know, and if I ask her, is it PMT, she storms out and slams the door—"

And then Kok Cheong says, "You know, that night at the beach, that was the best night of my life."

Tom is deliberately non-committal: "Uh huh," he says, or, occasionally exerting himself, "Gosh." He feels no obligation to be even minimally consoling; he has not sought out these confidences.

He does not tell Christie what Kok Cheong has said, and he does not tell Kok Cheong what Christie has said. He feels all the power and helplessness of an intermediary, caught in the middle of these telephonic dances; he feels, fleetingly, criminal.

Perhaps he simply likes betrayal. Perhaps he should have been a spy.

• • •

They go out once in a while, the three of them, always to pubs, discos, where the noise is such that any sort of normal conversation is impossible. The threesome is usually at Kok Cheong's insistence; he wants Tom along as an ally, Tom knows, a sort of silent witness to the incipient blood-letting which he feels, prophetic, to be in the air. As for himself, he derives a sort of perverse pleasure from the knowledge that when he goes back, he will call Christie, or she will call him. Kok Cheong's blindness makes him seem touching, almost lovable, in need of protection, a thing he hadn't thought possible.

Christie talks to Tom on the phone but she is sleeping with Kok Cheong. Or, has slept with him. Tom guesses this, from what he knows of Kok Cheong ("It takes two to tango" is one of his more infamous sayings) and from their showy physical intimacy in public. They are constantly nuzzling, reclining against each other, lacing and unlacing hands: Tom could have given them marks for the whole panoply which, he feels with some paranoia, has been put on specially for his benefit. Or he could be imagining things: his frame of mind is such that he imagines conspiracies, treacheries, where there are none.

Now and then Christie looks at him, mutely challenging; she is contemptuous of him, for sitting there, stolid and unbudgeable. "Voyeur," she says to him over the phone. "Spectator." It is true. He plays with his glass, looks round for people he knows, while all the time violent, unreal thoughts run through his head, thoughts of smashing the glass, digging the fragments into his palm.

Kok Cheong is trying to tell a funny story about medical school, something about a severed arm being missing from the mortuary. How a severed arm had then turned up in the locker of an unpopular student called Cheng, everybody assuming that it was a cruel, but fitting, prank. How it turned out that the severed arm was not in fact the missing limb at all, and nobody could figure out whose it was—

"Excuse me," Tom says, and runs for the bathroom.

He makes up his mind never to go out with them again.

• • •

The worst thing about love, Tom decides, is that it ruins your concentration.

Ragged, he hasn't opened a textbook in weeks. He skips lectures or doodles his way through them, his mind a blank. He can't even feign much interest when Animal manages to dig up a bootleg Jimi Hendrix record on which he has blown his life's savings. He stops calling Christie, and stops taking her calls; yet he waits, obsessively, for the phone to ring. His body and joints ache, for no apparent reason.

Hamzah and Animal suspect something is wrong. He has been downcast; he broods; he sings Speedy Gonzalez with such a tragic air that customers have inquired whether he is ill. The management threatens a termination of contract unless the act picks up. Froth and energy, though, are things Tom is currently deficient in.

"Forget her," Hamzah says, brutally. He delivers a stirring little homily along the lines of "plenty of fish in the ocean," etc., etc. All very well, Tom thinks, but what does one do if one's irrational hankering is for a particular fish?

He hears things. That Kok Cheong and Christie have had a public, enthralling row; that they have broken up; that they have made up; that she is seeing someone else; that he is seeing someone else; the gossip and the malice ebb and flow, as regular and cyclical as the tide—they are, after all, one of the more colourful couples on campus.

Once, he runs into Kok Cheong at the university tennis courts. Kok Cheong looks wrecked, beady-eyed, hungover. In answer to Tom's queries, he replies, abstractedly, "Fine, fine," and challenges Tom to a tennis match; he won't take no for an answer. Tom is pulverised: Kok Cheong plays like a demented hare, chasing every ball and giving uncharacteristic whoops whenever he hits a winner. Later, he asks Tom, not looking at him, "Have you heard from Christie?" Tom says, truthfully, "No." Kok Cheong nods, morosely, and walks off without another word, batting a tennis ball over his shoulder as he does so. Tom's hand flies out, mechanically, to catch it. Fellow sufferers, he thinks, we should get together and commiserate; he ought to relish the irony in it, but he doesn't. He gives the tennis ball to a child who has wandered on court.

• • •

"What a surprise," Kok Cheong says, flatly.

Christie is sitting by his hospital bed, biting her nails. She looks up as Tom steps into the room, bearing a basket of fruit. Tom stops short; he didn't expect to find her here, in the role of solicitous bedside companion. He hasn't seen her in weeks, and the vividness of her presence is like a slash, cutting him anew. He judges from their faces that they are not enthralled to see him. "Hey, I can come back," he says.

"Sit down," Kok Cheong says. "Join the party."

Kok Cheong has had a serious accident. A few days ago, he crashed his car through the central reservation barrier on the expressway, crumpling the front of the car like a concertina. He is listed in a stable condition at Mount Elizabeth, where his hamster-loving heart specialist father works. Christie was also in the car, but escaped largely unscathed, except for a few minor bruises.

Kok Cheong says, "Boy, do I feel stupid." From his bed, he looks from one to the other, turning his head slowly, painfully; his glance has a searching, unsettling quality.

Christie stays silent, so Tom says, "Why?"

"Crashing my car. Being a cliché. That's part of it."

The scene, the tableau, is somehow unreal, Tom feels. It is as if he and Christie have deliberately contrived this meeting, this opportunity to gaze at each other theatrically across the poor, mutilated body of the sacrificial victim, except that the sacrificial victim is refusing to collude and is, in fact, radiating a distinctly prickly hostility.

"Yes, I feel stupid," Kok Cheong says, ruminatively. "I've come to realise certain things. Christie knows what they are."

"Don't start," Christie says.

"I'm not starting anything. In fact, that's the whole problem, right? Endings. We're talking about endings here. Or am I wrong?" No one contradicts him.

And then he closes his eyes, suddenly. "I'm tired," he

says. It is a dismissal. They stand and leave the room, like disciplined children.

"Thanks for the fruit," Kok Cheong says.

• • •

Outside, Tom says, "What was that all about?"

"Oh, don't pretend," she says, angrily. "Don't pretend you don't know."

"No," Tom says. "I *don't*?"

She starts to cry, standing there in the hospital corridor. It is a kind of crying he has never seen before, a furious, hate-filled stream of tears, completely silent, while she looks at him, steadily, as if she could kill him.

• • •

Of course, he guesses by now what must have happened. Accidents have causes; it's simply a matter of tracing them back to the one definitive, irreducible moment, the one when a teleologist says, "Yes, that's when the Universe began." It could have been the fact that she chose to tell Kok Cheong, in the car, that she was leaving him, which decision Kok Cheong refused, stubbornly, to accept, without an interrogation as to the rival whom he persisted in believing had cut him out, running through a list of potential swains, each more preposterous than the last, while Christie issued her denials, wearily, then with increasing fury. Then it must be Tom, Kok Cheong said, expecting incredulity, hilarity, until he saw by her face that none of these were forthcoming; and, in the fraction of a second that he took his eyes off the road, he lost control of the car. It could have been any of those facts; or none of them.

"It's funny, isn't it," Christine is saying. "I know everybody is going to think I was somehow to blame for the accident. That I provoked him or something. When the truth is, there was no causal connection at all."

She looks at him, wanting affirmation as to the arbitrariness of life and death, wanting absolution. He wants to say he is not the person to give it, but he cannot bear her supplicating tone, so unlike her, and so he says, no, there was no connection at all. He senses the relief in her, while fear rises in him, setting the ends of his nerves on fire: he knows, as sure as he has ever been of anything, that they are bound together inextricably by this.

• • •

"You live here?" Tom says.

She nods, impatiently. She has already paid the taxi-driver and clambered out, while he is still looking out at a block of pre-war flats.

"I thought you were rich," he says, wondering, following her past an overflowing rubbish truck above which flies buzz, luxuriantly, and up a dark hallway lit by a single bulb. She gives him a scornful look; she seems to have recovered, during the long, silent ride back.

The flat is small, and cluttered. Vases, books, news-papers, bits of cloth, stationery, lie jumbled together on the shelves, also plates of half-eaten, moulding food, he cannot help noticing. Two large armchairs, smothered in moth-eaten antimacassars, take up most of the space in the living room. The TV is an old black and white set that stands on an upturned box against one wall. One shelf is given over to dozens of photographs in rusting frames: sepia-coloured, stiffly-posed, curling at the edges, they are of some antiquity. He examines them, while Christie flies about, tidying up, emptying plates, wiping, straightening.

The photographs show a polyglot of races: an Edwardian man with a walrus moustache; a young woman in a Peranakan blouse; an Indian man in a 1920s duck suit and spats. The more recent ones show Christie as a child, suspended between two adults, her parents, he supposes; by then the ethnic blend is so complete it is impossible to tell the origins of these three people, assuming anyone thought it interesting. Tom does; he has always been curious about the genealogy of Eurasians; it has always been an unconscious, heretical regret of his that he is, unexcitingly, only Chinese.

"These are your parents?"

"They died in a plane crash when I was two," Christie says. "I never knew them."

"Then who...?"

The unspoken question is answered by a tentative, "Christie?" and an elderly woman comes into the living room, blinking at the light. She is small and stooped and very frail; as she settles into one of the massive armchairs, she seems to be swallowed up in the upholstery, a tiny floral dot against the cerise leather. Her hair is completely white. "Hello, Auntie," Christie says. "Some tea?"

"Yes please, dear," the old lady says. She gives her hand, trustingly, to Tom, as though extending an audience. She seems not to notice that it is past midnight and that Christie has brought a strange young man to the flat.

• • •

The kettle comes, wailing, to the boil, and Christie makes three cups of tea. Great-aunt Eugenia is handed a plate of biscuits and this she puts decorously on her lap, nibbling at each biscuit with tiny, mouse-like movements. She talks about her childhood during the 1920s.

"We were well-off then," she says, regally, to Tom. "We had a house in Nassim Road, and every weekend there were parties. My mother loved fancy dress parties. She would dress up in silk and feathers and beads and I would help her. All gone now, of course. My father drank, you see. Then the Depression came, and the War, and we shed the house, and the servants, until one day there were none at all and my poor mother had to do her own washing."

Tom straddles a hard-chair brought out from the kitchen. He glances across at Christie, wondering whether she has heard these stories before. Christie looks impassive, walled-in, her eyes fixed on her great-aunt; he cannot tell what she is thinking. It seems very quiet, except for Great-aunt Eugenia's spidery, rhythmic voice, a voice from the past. He has a sudden vision of Kok Cheong lying in the hospital bed, connected to various tubes and catheters and wires, no, they are growing out of him, he is sprouting them, organic stems and roots and tendrils, forming a flowerbed. He gives himself a little shake; he needs to sleep, badly; it has been a long day.

"Can we put the television on, Christina?"

"They've stopped broadcasting, Auntie."

"Strange." She turns to Tom. "I've forgotten his name," she says to Christie, puzzled, her young-old face uplifted expectantly.

"Tom," Christie says, patiently, for the fifth time. She has the briskly efficient manner of a nurse with her great-aunt—kindly, firm, but never really listening to the patient.

"I think," says Great-aunt Eugenia, "I should like to go to bed."

She wedges the plate with its heap of biscuit crumbs between two books on the nearest shelf, extends her hand again to Tom, and vanishes into her room. The door closes with a soft click.

• • •

"She took me in after my parents died, and brought me up. Two years ago, she had a stroke, and her memory has been failing ever since." They are in Christie's room, a Spartan affair. The bed is an ancient, creaky metal contraption like the ones in army barracks; a single chair stands beside it. A small table doubles as a desk and a dresser. He knows now where she derives her lack of sentimentality from, the capacity he has glimpsed in her for making a clean severance at the root in all matters.

Christie lights up and sits hunched on the bed, knees drawn up to her chin. She holds her hand out for the ashtray; he hands it to her.

"You smoke too much."

"You've said that before."

Her bed is hard and springy, uncomfortable; he cannot imagine that she has been sleeping in it all these years. He unfurls her legs and she flops back, the hand holding the cigarette raised above her head to avoid singeing the bedclothes. Ash scatters in an arc on the pillow. Arms propped on the bed, he lies on top of her, length to length, a pair of cards. He runs his finger along her cheekbones and removes her cigarette.

"I'm not rich," Tom says, temporizing. "I don't think I ever will be."

"Pity," Christie says, drily, a little wistfully, he thinks. Then she asks, "Do you think we'll pay for this?"

He reminds her, "There's no causal connection." Then he says, incorrigible honesty getting the better of him, "Yes, probably, but who cares." He has to ask as well, the thing that has been bothering him for weeks, "Why me?"

In answer, she touches his face.

Hell Hath No Fury

The road to Damascus for Grandma occurred on a hot Sunday morning in the church of St. Aloysius, Roman Catholic, ten-thirty A.M. Father Le Mesurier, the old French priest who normally conducted Mass in a thickly incomprehensible French accent, was away on holiday. In his place was Father James Hsien, newly graduated from a Taiwanese seminary.

Father Hsien was so short that nobody in the congregation realised he had streamed in until an admonitory reedy voice piped over the sound system, "Brothers and sisters in Christ, PLEASE STAND!" Startled, the congregation leapt to its feet. Over the top of the lectern, the beginnings of a crew cut and thick tortoiseshell glasses of a type not seen since the 1950s could be glimpsed. From what they could see of him, he appeared to be all of twenty-one years old. (He was, in fact, ten years older). He looked like an infant swaddled in sacerdotal robes for a joke.

In his opening remarks, he told the assembled throng there was much sin about and little grace and redemption. With this unpromising start, he steamed into a sermon that managed to antagonise everybody from the large expatriate American community ("America is a land of sin and fornication, plagued by crime, drugs and Aids"), to the society ladies who organised charity lunches and thought themselves remarkably benevolent ("And I say to you, think of how you treat your maids. For the gospel says that the meek shall inherit the earth, so how will your diamonds, your cars and your travels avail you?"), to Grandma ("And I know of old ladies who waste their last years playing mahjong and living from one meal to the next, instead of reflecting on their sins and the life that is to come..."). With that last salvo, Grandma came awake with a look of murder on her face. It was all the Tan family could do to prevent her from marching up the aisle and clouting Father Hsien around the head with her handbag. Quivering with indignation, she refused to go for communion; she wanted nothing to do with "that man."

On the ride home, she fulminated against the Catholic Church, its bossy patriarchy and above all Father Hsien. "I should never have sent you to the convent," she told her daughter, Mrs Tan. "I should have known that colonial institution would have you rushing into the church. What does that man know about anything? He's still wet behind the ears. I've given birth to six children—"

"Mother," said Mrs Tan, patiently, "I don't think he was referring to you personally."

"He was looking," said Grandma, "right at me."

Her grandchildren, Peter and Jonathan (good Biblical names) groaned. Mr Tan drove on with a long-suffering look on his face. He was thinking that if Father Hsien managed to wean his mother-in-law off her marathon nocturnal mahjong sessions, he would, like a good disciple, drop all and follow him. Not exactly drop *all*, of course, but he would certainly be a lifelong devotee. Mr Tan was an engineering lecturer with a propensity towards migraines who craved above all peace, quiet and tranquillity. There was very little of any with his mother-in-law around.

The next Sunday Grandma announced that she was a fully paid-up member of the Renewal Charismatic Free Church for All Brethren. She had washed her hands of the Catholic Church.

• • •

"She's joined *what*?" said Mr Tan.

Mrs Tan, close to hysterics and convinced her mother was doomed to hellfire, repeated the name of the church. Again, Mr Tan, good at engineering terms and bad at civilian discourse, missed it by a mile.

"Oh," he said.

"It's one of those fundamentalist Protestant groupings where they speak in tongues and insist that everyone pays ten per cent of their income."

"She hasn't got an income."

"That's not the point. The point is, she's been led astray."

"Oh, now really," said Mr Tan. "We all believe in the same things in the end."

"No, they don't. They don't believe in the Virgin Mary or acknowledge the Pope or—this is *horrible*."

As it turned out, Grandma had very little idea what her new brethren *did* believe in. She had joined the renegades because her friend Mrs Sinnathuray was a member and because the pastor, the Reverend Michaels from Peoria, Illinois, was so handsome and so kind. Not at all like the vituperative dwarf at St. Aloysius. And she liked the rousing services, where there was a good deal of arm-waving, breast-beating and being born again. ("Everything short of Mardi Gras," said a distraught Mrs Tan.) So very different from the Catholic Church, where people slumbered through Mass in an agreeable stupor and had only the foggiest notion of the Bible's contents. Grandma, in a most moving personal testimony to a packed assembly, laid the blame for her years of waste and error squarely at the door of the Pope.

But Grandma was nothing if not broadminded. She went right on reciting her rosaries and praying to the Virgin Mary. And her mahjong parties increased in bonhomie and amplitude, as her new church members took to her like ducks to water, in spite of her theological shakiness.

"*So* delightful!" they said to Mr Tan. "At her age, with her energy, her mind, remarkable!"

Mrs Tan resolutely stayed in her room during these proceedings. When she did appear, she drifted through, wraith-like, hollow-eyed. The Brethren left her alone, recognising that here was a woman who had closed her mind to the Message. Mr Tan's chief emotion at these times was a wishful desire that his wife would stand up to her mother, but that, he knew, was beyond her. It was beyond him, for that matter. Grandma was an Act of God.

However, no matter how much the Brethren smiled, chirped and wolfed down the food in the refrigerator, they never shook off the air they carried with them of venturing into the home of infidels and pagans. Mr Tan recognised the familiar battle-light gleaming in the eye of the keen proselytiser as, one by one, they bore down on him.

"Don't you want," they invariably began, "to join a church where you feel you belong, where you know you're at home?"

Mr Tan, a man of limited spiritual needs, felt his head beginning to throb. They wouldn't leave him alone in the office and now they were invading his home as well. "I do go to church," he pointed out.

They smiled disbelievingly. They never stopped smiling, but there was a range of meanings compressed into those smiles. This was the gently humouring smile. Did the secret of their success lie in those never ending, fixed smiles? Come to think of it, Catholics generally went around dour and indifferent, hardly beacons of light for their faith.

"We believe," they said, "in a participatory church. Where you take part in a service that glorifies God. We don't believe in passively following ritual."

Mr Tan waved a feeble hand at his sons, returning noisily after football practice. It was a signal for help but they ignored him. "Gosh, hi, Dad, bye, Dad," they said. "Got to rush, Dad." They bolted themselves in their room.

Mr Tan was not a particularly religious man. It had to do with the fact, he sometimes thought, that he was a man of little imagination; the thought of death, the afterlife, the sense of a higher, divine being, seldom disturbed him. He wasn't given to asking why. He was a Catholic by marriage and that, it seemed to him, was as good a reason as any. The histrionics, the sheer *energy* involved in becoming a born-again Christian, appalled him. And there were times when he told himself that if the Europeans hadn't flooded Asia with their missionaries and their schools, he would still be a Buddhist, comfortably subsisting in the darkness where there was supposed to be weeping and gnashing of teeth. What if the so-called act of faith was nothing but a historical accident?—He realised, with relief, that it was time to go to bed.

• • •

Grandma's rebirth was akin to lobbing a stone into a still pond: it created ever-widening ripples. One of its immediate effects was that Grandma became tremendously interested in the Apocalypse and the Antichrist.

"You will know the end of the world is nigh," she reported, "when there are earthquakes, famines and volcanic eruptions."

"They've always been around," Mr Tan said dampeningly.

Grandma gave him a shirty look. "The point is," she said, "that we always have to be ready, no matter where we are or what we're doing. Imagine! If the Lord came to earth while I was in the bathroom, what would I do?" (Nobody could find a ready answer to this either.)

Then she discovered that the Proctor & Gamble trademark was thought by some to be depicting the Antichrist. She hot-footed it home, determined to eradicate all use of their products, but *everything* in the nature of a cleansing agent was apparently manufactured by P & G or a subsidiary. This struck Grandma as even more sinister. How could a single multinational have a monopoly on all the soap circulating in the world?

"I guess it's a case of being clean or being pure,' Jonathan said. The whole family soaped away, P & G-style, doing its best to boost capitalist exploitation and ignoring Grandma's warnings.

Next, Grandma took it into her head that Ronald Reagan was the beast himself; 666 was the number of the beast, was it not, and there were six letters in each of his names. 'That only makes 66," Mr Tan pointed out; in spite of himself, he was becoming quite interested in all this.

'This is totally infantile," Mrs Tan declared. "Numerology under the guise of Christianity—honestly!"

There was nothing she could do, however, to stop Grandma from giving a delicious shudder every time the avuncular features of Mr Reagan appeared on the screen, or to prevent the boys from yapping and howling in dire imitation of a werewolf whenever his name was mentioned. Mrs Tan, who was supremely rational in every area outside Catholicism, told anyone who would listen that it was simply mind boggling that the man who had acted with Bonzo the Chimp could in any way be associated with the forces of evil. She was discovering the labyrinthine and peculiar byways of Christianity and they appalled her.

The next Sunday, Peter Tan, fifteen, electrified his family by announcing that he had became a Buddhist and wouldn't be attending Mass any longer. After a heated argument about transport convenience (the family usually went for lunch after Sunday Mass) he sulkily accompanied the rest to church.

Later, in his room, they discovered a book called *Zen and the Art of Motorcycle Maintenance*. "Have you been corrupted by this book?" Mrs Tan demanded.

Peter shrugged sleepily. He was tall for his age, slender, and surreptitiously growing his hair whenever his parents didn't notice. Dreamy and dissociated, his parents feared he might never become the lawyer/doctor/accountant/banker they wanted him to be. Jonathan, sixteen and aloof, said, distantly, "Don't ask *me*," when cornered. He was going through a family-phobic phase and his whole manner implied he was not his brother's keeper.

"*Why* are you doing this?" Mrs Tan asked her son, with a sort of petrified tranquillity.

"I just happen to find Buddhism a lot more compatible, Mum."

"Compatible!"

"Catholicism is a patriarchal and bureaucratic religion, Mum. It's drifted away from its roots. Sure, maybe it was a good idea in its time but Jesus would be horrified if he came down now and saw what his followers had done."

Mrs Tan made a gurgling, semi-strangled noise.

"Buddhism doesn't require any structures. That's the beauty of it. It's inner-directed. It's not egocentric. You can be a force for good wherever you are—"

"*Wah*, his language improve so very much, one, hor, when he become Buddhist, so funny, what, what," said Jonathan. His father told him not to be sarcastic. Ostentatiously, he joined the choir at St. Aloysius as head choirboy.

Meanwhile, Peter said that animals were as worthy, if not more worthy, of respect than old Homo sapiens and he was becoming a vegetarian. He prowled the neighbourhood collecting stray cats and dogs; he even launched a Stop Killing Flies campaign. At mealtimes, he lectured his family on the unsavoury practices of the meat industry, and one choice anecdote about veal in particular had Jonathan rushing to the bathroom. The odour of sanctity carried about him, the family felt, was positively sickening. "I hope you're reincarnated as a cockroach, so I can step on you," Jonathan told his brother; Peter flew across the room and landed on him—it took both their parents to tear them apart. The situation, it seemed, was rapidly approaching West Bank flashpoint level.

"This is all your fault," Mrs Tan said, between gritted teeth, to her mother. These days she went around in a frozen calm, a self-willed deep freeze which was rather alarming.

Grandma had the grace to look a trifle disconcerted. "I don't know what you mean."

"Yes, you do, Mother! You started a revolution! You're breaking up my home!"

"Such melodrama," said Grandma, briskly. She skipped out, nimbly, with a little stack of pamphlets titled, Get On The Nearest Hotline To God! (blue covers for non-Christians, red covers for Catholics). She was going to the City Hall MRT station to distribute them to the uninitiated.

"If she gets picked up by the police and spread all over the front pages, I'm renouncing her as my mother-in-law," Mr Tan said.

"This is *not* funny," said his wife.

Just then, the Reverend Michaels arrived.

• • •

It was with some difficulty that Mrs Tan could be dissuaded from slamming the door in his face. She considered him the author of, the perpetrator behind, her mother's behaviour. This large, corn-fed American with the very blue, porcelain eyes and the very white teeth, who did he think he was, leaving America to spread mayhem and dissension in once united families? She looked at him with the sort of defiance that the Catholic

Mary Queen of Scots must have brought with her to the gallows, or was it the executioner's chopping block? She couldn't remember.

"Ah, Mrs Tan," said the Reverend Michaels. He took both her hands in his. It was the first time she had met him face to face since she had hitherto assiduously avoided him. He had a long, slow drawl, and a brilliant smile. He wore a short-sleeved, open-necked shirt, undone to the second button, above which tufts of luxuriant chest hair could be seen, and a pair of Levi's 501 chinos. He was very good-looking—this knowledge slowly filtered through the haze of indignation with which she regarded him. (Also the fact that his size twelve feet draped all over the front doorstep made it impossible to dislodge him.)

"It's so *varry*, *varry* nice to meet you, Mrs Tan," said the Reverend Michaels.

"Your mother has told me *so* much about what a wonderful daughter you are, Mrs Tan," the Reverend Michaels added.

By this time, he had somehow insinuated himself into the front hall and seated himself in an armchair in their living room, legs crossed, beaming in response to a somewhat dazed offer of a drink from Mrs Tan.

"Just water, if you please, ma'am. The religious life is such thirsty work."

Left alone, the Reverend Michaels and Mr Tan contemplated each other's knees. Mr Tan had met him before and had found the charisma somewhat overpowering, like musk. "Do you—er—often wear jeans?" he asked feebly.

The Reverend Michaels laughed genially. "They're my disguise," he confided, "for slipping in behind enemy lines, you know. Folks see a guy in jeans, they figure he can't be a minister and that lowers their guard. The only problem," he said thoughtfully, "are the girls. Young girls, especially."

"Have to beat them off with a stick, eh?"

The Reverend Michaels dug him in the ribs and grinned. "*Exactly.*"

Mrs Tan returned with a glass. "What can we do for you?" she asked, somewhat abruptly; in the kitchen she'd had time to recover from the impact of the gaze from those eyes. "I'm afraid my mother's not in."

"*Wa-al*, actually, I was rather hoping she wouldn't be. You see, it's like this." He leaned forward, clasping his hands earnestly. "Your mother wants to donate a large, antique lacquered table to our church, to function as an altar. Now, under normal circumstances, I'd be more than happy to accept it—more than happy. As you know, we're desperately in need of what businessmen call startup capital." Flash of teeth. "We're a fledgling church and we welcome all the donations we can get—"

"Wait a minute," said Mr Tan. He turned to his wife. "Isn't that the antique table she promised to leave us in her will?" (They'd had it valued some years ago: the expert had put it at a conservative estimate of $10,000.)

Mrs Tan nodded, distracted by the slender golden hairs, glistening in the sunlight from the window, on the Reverend Michaels' wrists.

"Are you aware," demanded the Reverend Michaels solemnly, "that it has an emblem of a Chinese dragon on the surface? In gold leaf?"

"Yes, of course. It's a very good example of the art flourishing in that period..." To think of the legacy, which they had always taken for granted, going to this man made Mr Tan feel faint. Not for the first time, he thought his mother-in-law ought to be certified.

"But we can't accept it," said the Reverend Michaels sorrowfully.

"Oh," said Mr Tan, taken aback.

From the depths of his armchair, the Reverend Michaels rose to a rhetorical splendour. "How can we start a church, sir, tainted with symbols of a pagan culture? Of a pagan civilisation? Our mission is to rid the world of superstition and fear and let the light flood in. To accept such an object would be the sheerest of bad luck." He realised what he had just said and laughed, uproariously. "Oh my, I've cooked my own goose, haven't I? *Wa-al*, you know what I mean."

"My mother will be disappointed," said Mrs Tan. Her husband looked at her, wondering; she was speaking in a peculiar, constricted tone of voice.

"We aim," said the Reverend Michaels, "not to please, but to do the right thing." He spread his hands, disarmingly. "We need an altar table, ma'am. Just not one with a dragon. You *will* let her know? Thank you.—And have you thought of joining your mother, and coming down to one of our gatherings?"

"Not exactly." Desperately, she focused her eyes on a point beyond him; she had the sensation of drowning.

"I understand you're a Catholic, but, please, don't be put off, we welcome everybody. As I said, we're a new church, but we're dedicated. Dedication is the word. We demand a huge commitment but we also give a lot back..."

When he was gone, an hour later, Mrs Tan rushed to her bedroom and sank to her knees. For once, praying had little effect, however; instead she splashed water on her temples and paced about angrily, telling herself to calm down and not to behave like an infatuated school-girl. For she had a weakness for terribly good-looking men in the old-fashioned mould, which forty-odd years of living had failed to dampen. One would have thought that at her age, with two teenage sons, she would get over these attacks, which left her suffused with confusion and a burning sense of embarrassment, but no, here she was flushing again. She tried to invoke the image of her husband, placidly going through the Sunday papers in the next room, but she could only dredge up a blank. He was the ideal husband: he was safe, steady, constant and never caused her the slightest anguish. Truth to tell, he was rather dull. She smacked her forehead in despair. "Jesus, Mary, Joseph,' she said aloud.

"Where are you off to?" queried her husband, as she tore through the sitting room, jangling the car-keys.

"I'm going to Mass."

He grunted. He was used to his wife's piety. As far as

he was concerned, all that mattered was that the legacy was safe.

• • •

Grandma returned with Mrs Sinnathuray at ten P.M., victorious. They had pinned various quivering youths to the wall of the station and had refused to let them go until they promised to attend the next service at the Free Church. "I tell you, I'm having more fun every day since my husband died," Mrs Sinnathuray declared.

"Oh, the Reverend Michaels was here today," said Mr Tan.

Grandma sat up straighter. "Really? What for?"

He told her.

Grandma's eyes snapped. "We'll see about that," she said. She strode to the telephone and called the church; it was true. Grimly, she replaced the receiver. "Oh, darling," said Mrs Sinnathuray despondently. She recognised all the familiar warrior symptoms in her old friend.

"Mother, you promised that table to us," Mrs Tan protested.

"Yes, I know, but it's a question of who has the greater need. You and the children are comfortably off. The church is just starting. I can't tell you how *exciting* it all is."

"Mother, the Reverend Michaels has said he doesn't want it."

"That's what he thinks."

"Mother, why are you *doing* this?"

"The Greeks called it hubris," Jonathan informed everyone. "We did it in literature."

Grandma launched herself into a flurry of activity. She decided that the thing to do was to get signatures for a petition urging the inclusion of the table, but she ran into some unexpected opposition. A few people—unbelievably—shared the Reverend Michaels' reactionary views on Chinese dragons. "Philistines," fumed Grandma. "What about St. George and the Dragon? I've never heard anyone objecting to that."

That, it transpired, was because St. George's Dragon was impeccably English, a well-established part of myth and folklore and the traditions of the early church. But, in any case, the Free Church frowned upon St. George and his unfortunate Dragon, seeing that the pair of them were so bound up with the fossilised structures and rigidity of High Church Anglicanism, which, after Catholicism, was Public Enemy Number Two in the Free Church's impressive canon of objects of vilification.

"It's just a dragon," insisted Grandma. The table, after all, would be covered with a clean white cloth during the service and nobody would have to view the offending beast. In Grandma's opinion, this refusal to accept her table was nothing less than a personal insult. Her weekly mahjong parties for the faithful lost some of their sparkle, as members took sides for and against the issue; there was a positively un-Christian tinge of rancour in the atmosphere.

"Hell hath no fury like that of one Christian loathing another," Jonathan said sagely.

The Reverend Michaels tried to reason with Grandma. He sat her down in his office, fed her biscuits and turned on her the full blast of his charm. He showed her pictures of himself as an angelic little boy in Peoria, Illinois, and of his favourite spaniel, Pooch. He told her she was invaluable, *invaluable*, in the church.

"But do you remember, ma'am," he said, earnestly, "the day you testified that you had become a new person? When you promised to sublimate your will to that of the Holy Spirit?" He was walking back and forth across the carpet, fists clenched to emphasise his point. Grandma nodded, mesmerised.

"Far be it that I should try to tell you what to do. *I* can't do it; only *you* can decide for yourself what action to take. The Good Lord gave us free wills to distinguish us from the animals so that we might exercise them. But there are ways and there are ways of using our talents." He perched on the arm of her chair, smiling beatifically down at her.

At this point, Grandma's resolution wavered a little. But then she caught sight of the good-humoured look in those cornflower-blue eyes, the serene conviction that *he*, Edward Danforth Michaels (a man to whom no one, and certainly no woman, had ever said no), would prevail. And the contrariness that coursed through her veins as surely as blood ever did led her to whip out the petition once again, and draw his attention to the two hundred and fifty signatures. The Reverend Michaels, his smile fading, stood, and pressed the tips of his fingers together, unavailingly. He pursed his lips; he was vexed, most vexed, and he made the mistake of saying so. They parted burgeoning enemies.

Finally, Grandma hit on a brainwave. She would hire a furniture removal company to transport the table to the church and install it while the Reverend Michaels was out fulfilling his pastoral duties. Presented with a fait accompli, he could hardly object, could he? She confided her plan to her supporters, a militant group who wanted the Reverend to take a more aggressive approach towards proselytising, and were exasperated by his high-charm, low-ferocity tactics. They saw this as a good way of registering disapproval.

So it happened that on a cloudy Friday afternoon, while the Reverend Michaels was conducting an infants' class at the home of a member, a large furniture truck rolled up to the front entrance of the church, Grandma ensconced in the front seat beside the driver, to whom she recounted the whole affair in high-velocity Hokkien. She felt like a military leader commanding a convoy. A dozen or so of her supporters milled around, hindering rather than helping in the unloading of the table. Grandma's mood was triumphal, imperial—first the table, then ... the possibilities were endless.

"*What* is the meaning of this?"

The drawl, the lilting cadence, was the same, but the geniality was gone. The Reverend Michaels hove into view, blond, Nordic, towering. There was a stunned silence. A frisson ran through the assembled rebels; what was he doing here? (They discovered later that he had dismissed the infants' class early.) As he came towards them in a furious rush, the thought that was uppermost in their minds was that he looked as if he were the wrath of God personified. They fell back on either side to let him through—someone remarked later that it was eerily reminiscent of the parting of the Red Sea. He stood before the table, heaving; out of nowhere, it seemed, he produced a stick and—everyone gasped—thrashed the delicate curved legs of the table. With an almighty, ominous CRACK, it settled down with a thump, a good five inches shorter. Then the Reverend Michaels, without so much as a backward glance, vanished, leaving a distinctly post-apocalyptic flavour in the air.

$$\bullet \; \bullet \; \bullet$$

Grandma took to her bed for a week. (The table, sent to the workshop, cost several thousand dollars to repair; the bill was duly despatched to the Renewal Charismatic Free Church for All Brethren.) The Tans, victorious but feeling it unseemly to crow, wore the mantle of quiet dignity as they tiptoed through the house. The mahjong parties ceased; the Brethren scattered their spiritual largesse elsewhere. Peter met a Catholic girl from the convent school down the road, and thought, perhaps, that Buddhism, well, wasn't exactly meant for him. The next Sunday, the whole family was back at St. Aloysius, Grandma barely blinking an eyelid while Father Hsien expatiated on the theme of spiritual pride. Her spirit was broken, her flesh subdued.

"I *told* you there was no need to panic," Mr Tan said to his wife.

That's what *you* think, she thought privately, though she did not answer. Absently, she fingered the crucifix around her neck. One needed a very strong faith to get through life.